Sixteen Steps to Fall in Love

Three Rivers Ranch Romance™

Book 15

Liz Isaacson

ISBN-13: 978-1-63876-296-6

"And be ye kind one to another, tenderhearted, forgiving one another, even as God in Christ forgave you."

Ephesians 4:32

Chapter One

Boone Carver yawned and stretched from his perch on the edge of his bed. From the other room, dog collars jingled and jangled as his bulldog and his yellow lab heard him and came running.

"Hey, guys." Amidst slobber from Lord Vader's jowls and tail whipping from Princess Leia's overactive rump, Boone scrubbed down the dogs. "You ready to run this morning?"

Of course they were. His dogs loved running almost as much as Boone did. The annual Amarillo Marathon was only eight short months away, and he was determined to be ready this year. His muscles ached a bit from his long run yesterday, coupled with the late shift at the animal clinic where he worked. They stayed open until eight on Thursdays, and while that didn't normally faze Boone, the five a.m. alarm to put in ten miles before breakfast certainly did.

He reminded himself that it was almost the weekend and he didn't have to work this one. He would be on call, but most people didn't call into the animal hospital unless there was a real emergency.

Dressed, stretched, and properly hydrated, Boone set out with Vader and Leia leashed beside him. Leia always tried to bolt out of the gate, and he had to hold her back, save some of his energy for mile six, when the fatigue would really hit him.

Boone lived on the northeast edge of Three Rivers, one of the last houses before the road stretched and went out to Three Rivers Ranch, where he worked also part-time.

He timed his breathing, measured his steps, and enjoyed the early summer morning air. It smelled like apples and pollen, and Boone relished in this town, this place he'd come to find sanctuary at a time he'd had none.

He passed an older gentleman walking a Boston terrier, and Boone lifted his hand in greeting. He'd seen that dog in the clinic a few months ago. Cracked paw pads. Looked like the dog had fully healed, and Boone's spirits soared. With his mind on work, he ran through the late-night paperwork he'd completed.

He'd gone over it three times, determined not to give any more ammunition to the office administrator who'd been in his face since the day he'd arrived at the clinic. If his handwriting wasn't "atrocious" and "illegible" then he'd forgotten to check some microscopic box on the sixteenth line on page three of a form. If not that, then he'd misspelled something so important Nicole Hymas had to tell the entire staff of his incompetence.

He'd laughed it off all while shooting her his most lasered looks. Over the past several months, though, he'd decided to make more of an effort to hide his dyslexic tendencies. Last night, he'd even erased an entire paragraph and rewritten it so she'd be able to read it more easily.

He wasn't sure why Nicole disliked him so much. Messy handwriting came with the territory of a doctor, right?

Yes, definitely, he told himself as he hit the Six-Mile Wall. Thankfully, he spent part of his time out at Three Rivers, so he didn't have to deal with Nicole and her surliness on Mondays or Wednesdays.

He approached the end of his run: a huge park, with public restrooms, statues, a fountain everyone threw coins in to make wishes, and a bark park—a fenced area just for the pooches. He unzipped his small backpack and pulled out the pop up bowl for his dogs and filled it with water. Lord Vader and Princess Leia drank greedily while Boone stretched and worked out the lactic acid in his muscles.

His running route on ten-mile days took him around Three Rivers and always ended at this park. When the dogs had finished lapping at several bowls of water, he walked them over to the bark park, scanning the area now that the sun had painted the surroundings in golden rays of light.

Only a handful of people came to the park this early, and Boone knew almost all of them. He nodded and waved and smiled before opening the gate and unleashing his dogs. They'd just run for a while, but Boone liked this cooling down period at the pet park. Enjoyed talking to the people who shared his love of animals. Had even met his hiking partner and Friday night, game-watching best friend, Dylan Walker, at this park.

Almost everyone in town knew what he did for a living, and he often answered questions while he rubbed out his calves and rehydrated for the day.

Today, no one approached him, and he ripped open a protein bar from his pack. Leia scampered around with a little pug he'd never seen before, and he glanced around for the dog's owner.

It had to be the blonde-haired woman with her back to him. He wondered if her almost white-blonde hair came from a bottle, but it still reminded him a bit of his aunt's. This woman was bent over another dog, her hair loose and flowing in a curtain that hid her face.

She picked up the tiny dog she'd been ministering to and straightened, scanning the park for the little pug. She wore a pair of tight yoga pants over her petite frame, along with an oversized sweatshirt in the exact shade of purple that reminded him of the grapes that grew on his family's ranch down in Hill Country.

His heart pounded out the promise that she'd be his next date. He hadn't been out with a woman in a couple of months, having decided not to burn through all the available females in the town in under a year.

He'd been in Three Rivers now for twelve months and five days, and he thought he'd like to get to know this woman a little better. Maybe a *lot* better.

"Taz," she called, turning toward him.

Boone startled, and promptly told his pulse to settle back into its proper place. *Now.*

Because the owner of the pug was none other than Nicole Hymas, the office administrator at the animal clinic where he worked three days a week.

He sucked in a breath when her eyes landed on him. She froze too, her surprise quickly melting into the usual sour expression she wore whenever she looked at Boone.

"He's over there." He indicated where the fawn-colored pug played with Leia.

Nicole frowned as she followed his hand gesture. She carried a tiny apricot-colored poodle that quivered in her arms as she stepped closer and closer to where Boone stood, his bulldog panting at his feet.

"Is this your dog?" She indicated Lord Vader.

"And that one playing with yours. Taz, is it?" Boone had never interacted with Nicole in such a civil way. He didn't even know the woman came in packaging labeled "nice." She'd been nasty to him since day one, and he'd never known why. But now, he smelled something like mint and lemons, and she didn't have any tension in her face, and her eyes didn't look like they were about to scald him.

"Yes." She beamed down at the little dog in her arms. "And this is Valcor."

Boone laughed, the sound flying free up toward the clouds. "That doesn't seem to fit."

Nicole scowled, effectively silencing Boone's clumsy laugh. "Thanks." She strode back to where she'd been standing and retrieved a small pack, which she buckled around her waist. Boone tried not to notice how trim she was—how had he missed it before? He tried not to stare at the way her hair nearly reached the pack—how had he never known she possessed yards of such beautiful hair?

She tossed him a disgruntled look he was very familiar with before leashing the pug and leaving the bark park. Boone watched her go, dateless and wondering if he could ever do anything right in the woman's eyes.

Boone arrived at Puppy Pawz Animal Clinic a few minutes before nine, already tired and hoping Nicole had called in sick.

No such luck. The woman sat in her office, which bore

a large window that overlooked the lobby area, where a receptionist greeted customers when they arrived.

"Good morning, Boone," Joanne chirped, drawing Nicole's attention. She rolled her eyes and Boone wished he possessed a superpower that could melt glass.

"Morning," he said, moving past the reception desk and through the door where he'd bring dogs to be treated. He had an office too, thank you very much. No window facing the facilities, so he entered and closed the door behind him, giving himself the privacy he wanted. Browning grass stretched beyond the window facing the outdoors, and Boone wished he were out there instead of in here.

He sighed, recalling the fantasy. He loved his job. He just didn't love working with Nicole. Heck, he'd appreciate it if he even *liked* working with Nicole. And now his blunder at the bark park had added fuel to an already simmering fire.

"But Valcor is a really silly name for a five-pound poodle," he muttered to himself as he put his lunch in the mini-fridge in the corner. He'd see all the dogs and cats that came in today, and he always checked the animals in the shelter on Fridays as well.

He turned away from the window at the faint sound of a woman singing. Nicole. She walked around the clinic with lyrics under her breath or a hum in the back of her throat. Boone had never minded—until today. Now, the sound of her voice sent his nerves across a cheese grater.

Be nice, he coached himself as he shrugged into his lab coat and exited his office to take the sixteen steps out to the reception area to get the chart for his first pet—and where he'd see Nicole. He said sixteen times, once with every slow step, *be nice, be nice, be nice....*

Chapter Two

Nicole Hymas had woken with the song she now sang in the back of her mind. Every morning, without fail, she woke with a new song in her head. Sometimes a song from church—something the choir was working on. Sometimes a song she'd heard on the radio. Sometimes a childhood nursery rhyme.

No matter what it was, her song of the day stuck with her no matter what she was doing. Today's song was "Happy Birthday." She hated the song, especially because she'd just had her fortieth birthday, alone save for her aging parents.

Sure, her siblings had called, but more out of obligation than that they actually knew her or cared about her. She didn't blame them, not really. Her closest sibling in age was already fifty-one. Forty was no big deal. Her oldest brother had turned sixty last fall.

Nicole was a caboose baby, a child that had come along after her mom and dad thought their family was already complete. She still felt like that most days—an afterthought. She sighed as she finished checking the patient rooms, that sense of disquiet that had been raging in her for the past month since her birthday rearing its ugly head.

Help me make it through today, she prayed as she returned to her office. Then she'd at least have the weekend to figure out how to tolerate the man who'd rolled into town a year ago in his fancy black truck and stolen the clinic out from under her. It was a process she had to complete every couple of months as she found flaw after flaw in the gorgeous Boone Carver.

She almost scoffed at the ludicrous way she'd classified him as good looking. But he was. And he knew he was, which really put lemons in Nicole's stomach. She just needed to stop thinking about him. Just stop—which would be a lot easier if his bass voice didn't reach right into her office every time he called for an animal to "Come on back" with him.

Nicole adjusted the scrubs she wore, wondering for the millionth time why she didn't dress like the office administrator she was. Foolish hope, she supposed, but had never dared admit out loud. Plus, it made dealing with her mother's illness a lot easier once she left the clinic and returned to her childhood home to check on her parents.

She swiped her bangs out of her face, the air conditioning in the ancient building that housed the clinic clearly on the fritz again. "Joanne," she called. "Can you call the maintenance department about the air conditioner?"

"Already did," the redhead said, causing a smile to form on Nicole's face. Joanne reminded Nicole of herself. A real go-getter. Someone who'd started volunteering at the clinic and had never left. That thought erased the smile from Nicole's face, and she opened the budget spreadsheet she needed to finish before the fiscal year started at the beginning of July, just a few short weeks away.

She wasn't sure how much time had passed before Boone said, "How was my paperwork from last night?" He stepped all the way into her office, infusing the air with the scent of antiseptic and pine needles. An odd combination that satisfied Nicole nonetheless.

"I haven't looked at it yet."

He leaned against the wall and folded his arms, a frown marring his dark eyes and drawing his eyebrows down. He wore a full beard the color of chestnuts, and he kept his hair trim and neat on the sides, longer on the top. Nicole wanted to know what it would feel like to run her fingers through that hair, find out if it was a soft as it looked.

She swallowed, her imagination running wild again. She definitely needed a weekend to get Boone out of her system completely.

"I didn't mean to laugh at your dog this morning," he said, his voice low and barely reaching her ears. She was sure she hadn't heard him right. He'd never apologized for anything, ever. When he'd completely forgotten the paperwork for the vaccinations he administered? Nothing. When she had to track him down and ask him what some of his words were? Just daggered glares. When she asked him which box she should check for the pet insurance? Growls and stabby pointing.

And he hadn't really apologized this time either, though her mind flew back to their encounter at the dog park. He'd been wearing the flimsiest pair of shorts a man should be allowed to wear and a shirt that seemed two sizes too small and one of those compact hiking hydration backpacks. His dog had seemed very sweet and loyal, lying at Boone's feet, and her heart had softened for about sixty seconds.

Still, jerks could have loyal dogs too.

"It's fine," she said.

"What's with the name Valcor? Does it mean something to you?"

It did, but she didn't want to tell him about her mom's childhood dog, an Irish terrier that had been as sweet as the tea Nicole made every weekend. With her mom slipping further and further from her each day, Nicole needed something to hold onto. And if it was a silly dog's name, she'd take it.

"Did you need something?" she asked instead of answering his question.

He straightened, his presence powerful and potent in such a small space. She needed him to leave right now. "I just wanted to check—never mind." He turned and stormed out of her office, leaving behind his annoyance and the lingering scent of his woodsy cologne.

She focused back on her computer, mostly because Joanne had witnessed his departure and was now staring openly at Nicole with wide, green eyes. Finishing the budget was hopeless, because all Nicole could think about was how the Boone she'd seen at the dog park that morning was a completely different man than who strutted around here in that blasted white lab coat like he owned the place.

"He *does* own the place," she said under her breath, wishing the words weren't quite so bitter on her tongue.

SHE TRIMMED roses and rhododendrons with wild abandon, Boone's parting words to her haunting her like phantoms.

Want to meet at the dog park again tomorrow?

They hadn't agreed to meet today. Why did he use the word *again*?

Snip, snip, snip.

She collected all the flower heads in a ten-gallon bucket and dumped them in her green recycling can. Over and over she clipped and snipped and picked up the fallen heads until her entire backyard had been trimmed. Gardening had always soothed her. She didn't have the most beautiful backyard in the entire town for no reason. She'd won an award from the city council a few years ago, and she booked at least three weddings in her backyard every summer.

She braced the apple tree with the wayward branch with a two-by-four, and moved through her mini-orchard checking her pink lady and fuji apple trees, her apricots, and her fig trees. Along the back fence she had peaches and pears, and she checked the watering line there to make sure these trees got their fair share of moisture leading into the summer heat. She'd made the mistake before in under-watering, and that had meant a lot of cultivating and worrying to bring those trees back to fruition.

Nicole ran her fingers along the tree bark, comfort threading through her at the beauty she found in nature. She found blooms so pretty, the way a fruit formed from a flower fascinating, the way life kept chugging along hopeful.

She exhaled, wishing she had half the beauty of the rose bushes she so lovingly tended to. Wishing she had someone to take care of her when she felt rundown and droopy. Taz and Valcor stuck to the patio, where she had their outdoor bowls, houses for each of them though they shared Taz's, their cooling pads, and an assortment of outdoor furniture.

She got out the last of the sweet tea she'd brewed last weekend and stuck an organic meal in the microwave before taking everything out to the shady patio. This was the extent of the outdoors that Nicole liked, and she finally relaxed.

What time tomorrow? she texted to Boone, unsure of why she was perpetuating the conversation. When he'd asked at work, she'd said she'd text him later. That was why. Nicole did what Nicole said she'd do, whether that was stay in Three Rivers, where there were no prospects for her professionally or personally, to take care of her terminally ill mother, or send a text to a man she found infuriating and arrogant.

It's my rest day, so whenever.

Nicole had no idea what a rest day was, though she suspected the running clothes he'd been wearing that morning had something to do with it. Maybe a training schedule?

You tell me.

She didn't want to set the time. She wanted him to do it so she could say she couldn't make it. Or did she want to make it? She wasn't sure, and she reached back and undid the bun she'd kept her hair in all day, more confused than she'd ever been in her life.

Nine-thirty?

* * *

Nine-thirty came and went, and still Nicole couldn't get herself to leave the house. Taz sat by the front door, waiting with a doleful look in his puggy eyes ever since Nicole had put on her shoes. She paced from the living room to the kitchen and back. She'd poured herself into a tight pair of pants and covered all the parts of her body she disliked with an oversized hoodie. She could go. Taz loved the park, though going up the stairs made Valcor sleep for hours.

"Should we go?" she asked the dogs. Valcor whined. Taz flopped down and peered up at her through his eyelashes.

"You liked that other dog, didn't you? That's it. I can't keep you from your doggy friends." She collected her waist pack with Taz's ball, his lead line, and the pet waste bags. She shoved a handful of treats in her pocket and leashed Taz before scooping Valcor into her arms.

She made the several-blocks walk to the dog park in record time, arriving slightly sweaty and out of breath. She paused, trying to calm her heart rate as she looked for the tall frame of Boone.

He stood out among the other patrons at the park because of his beard and swoopy hair, both of which were extremely attractive to Nicole. She hadn't dated in years, and she didn't quite know what counted and what didn't.

She was at least twenty minutes late. Was this a date? Did people count a meeting at the bark park a date?

Might as well find out, she thought.

She watched Boone bend and pick up a ball before throwing it for his yellow lab, who sprinted after it with flapping ears. Nicole loosed Taz as soon as they went through the gate, and he sprinted toward Boone's dog.

Boone chuckled and leaned down to pat her pug, who flopped on the ground like Boone's hands were made of magic. Nicole had never been jealous of her dog before, but now she was. Her thoughts had turned traitorous on her.

Sure, maybe she'd thought about dating Boone before. He was a man—a single man, which wasn't that easy to come by in Three Rivers—and extremely good-looking. And a veterinarian who'd had enough money to buy the clinic. But she'd never actually thought anything would come of her schoolgirl crush.

And yet, there he was, glancing up and smiling at her like he was happy to see her. The song she'd woken up with paraded through her mind. *Jesus, take the wheel....*

She could definitely use some divine help about now, especially because her mouth had decided to betray her too by smiling back.

He stole your clinic, she told herself to cover up the loud lyrics. *He stole your clinic. He stole your clinic....*

Chapter Three

Surprise flitted through Boone. He hadn't expected Nicole to come to the dog park, though she hadn't exactly said she wouldn't. She hadn't said she would either, had never answered his text at all.

He wished he could say he didn't care. That the lack of her texting hadn't kept him up for an extra hour. But ever since yesterday morning, and all that delightfully buttery hair, Boone had been thinking about Nicole in a whole new way. It irked him that she hadn't even looked at the paperwork he'd taken such care with, but they weren't at work right now.

She wore her hair in a high ponytail, and he realized now that she always wore it in a bun at the clinic, which made it impossible for him to tell how long it was. She also always wore scrubs, though he wasn't sure why. She only worked with the animals in the shelter, not the pets who came in for treatment over in the hospital side, and she never gave shots or anything of the medical sort.

And she wasn't wearing scrubs today, but another pair of those tight pants, this time with a teal stripe down the side. She set her toy poodle in the grass, but it didn't move to run or play. When she stepped, so did the dog.

"All right," he told Leia and Taz. "Who wants to chase the ball?" He tossed it, sending both dogs after it, and turned back to Nicole. "It's good to see you."

"Yeah?"

Boone frowned at the incredulous tone in her voice and the way her eyebrows disappeared beneath her bangs.

"Outside of work," he said, trying to clarify what he meant.

Nicole just looked at him like he was speaking Japanese. He felt the same way, because he couldn't make his thoughts settle into anything coherent. Princess Leia returned with the ball, and Boone took the opportunity to move a couple of steps away from Nicole's intoxicating scent of minty lemons to throw the ball again.

"So what do you like to do outside of work?" he asked. "Besides come to the dog park, obviously."

Nicole tucked her hands into her hoodie, her shoulders bunched. She clearly wasn't comfortable with him, and he wracked his brain again for what he'd done to make her dislike him so much. And wasn't she hot in that sweatshirt?

"Gardening," she said just as Taz dropped a slobbery ball at her feet.

Boone watched Lord Vader as he went over to a much larger mastiff and started sniffing. He literally couldn't think of a single thing to ask her.

"What are your dog's names?" she asked.

"So that's Princess Leia," he said as his lab ran after the ball he threw. "And Lord Vader is over there, flirting with getting snapped at."

"Princess Leia and Lord Vader?" She giggled, and Boone had never heard such a sound from her. She was all business at work, and usually quiet and reserved. "Big Star Wars fan?"

"My father's a big fan." He shrugged. "I guess it rubbed off on me." Boone thought of his parents a bit further south in Texas Hill Country, his perfect older brother who worked the ranch, and his younger sister who taught school in the nearby town.

Only Boone had dared break the mold and leave town. Being a middle child wasn't easy, especially with a father who really wanted his children to leave a mark on the world. Boone wasn't sure how to do that, and his father's words followed him around like a wispy shadow.

"So what do you do besides running?" she asked.

He exhaled and chuckled. "Let's see. I grew up on a ranch, so I like to fish, and hunt, and hike. I'm training for the Amarillo marathon next year, so yes, I like to run. And I like taking care of animals."

"You're good at it."

"Is that a compliment?" He took a chance and looked fully at her, something he hadn't dared do quite yet. He laughed when her expression showed discomfort. Her hazel eyes sparkled, halfway between flirtatious and guarded.

"You already have a big enough head," she said. "You don't need compliments from me."

Boone fell back a step. "So you think I'm arrogant." He wasn't asking, and it wasn't the first time he'd been accused of such a trait. He didn't mean to come off that way, but somehow he did, at least to some people. Nicole, apparently.

"I didn't say that."

"You didn't need to." He whistled to his dogs, and they came running. They both sat in front of him and he treated them. "Time to go guys. Say goodbye to the other dogs and the pretty lady."

She locked her eyes on his. "Pretty?"

Heat crawled up his neck, and he shrugged again. "Sorry to make you come hang out with me when you clearly didn't want to."

He'd taken four steps away when she said, "I looked at your paperwork before I left last night."

He turned back toward her. "Yeah?"

"It looked good." She swallowed and clenched her arms tighter around her middle. "Thanks for doing that."

Boone, employing his bravery and taking a chance,

returned to her. Got right in close to her. "What did I do to you?"

She had to tilt her head back to look up at him. "What?"

"You've never liked me. I must've done something. What is it?"

Every defense she had—and probably some she didn't—flew into place. Her eyes closed off and her jaw clenched.

Boone smiled and backed away. "All right. But I'll find out." He needed to so he could fix it, because he was still interested in Nicole even though she emanated iciness, and he wanted to see if he could thaw her out.

"No, it's fine," Boone said into his phone on Sunday morning. "I'll be right over."

Pete Marshall wouldn't have called if it wasn't something important with one of his horses out at Courage Reins, a therapeutic riding facility on the same land as Three Rivers Ranch.

He picked up the plate containing his breakfast of eggs and cottage cheese and scooped half into Leia's bowl and half into Vader's. They slurped happily as scrambled eggs were one of their favorite foods and he shouldered one of his lab coats before leaving the house.

Boone pulled up the barn at Three Rivers Ranch,

taking an extra moment in his air conditioned cab before getting out. He took a deep breath, something about this ranch as soothing as the one he'd left in Grape Seed Falls.

He didn't want to own a ranch or work one. His older brother Dwayne did that and was remarkably good at it.

Boone was good at his job too, and he'd actually started asking his father for more and more advice about running a business since he'd bought Puppy Pawz ten months ago.

With a spark of realization, he realized he relied on Nicole to run the office and she was perfect at it. Maybe he needed to compliment her more. Let her know he appreciated what she did, that she hadn't even blinked when he'd come in as the new vet and then the new owner.

"There you are." Squire Ackerman, owner of Three Rivers Ranch and Boone's cousin, came out of the barn and shook Boone's hand.

"Somethin' smells good out here," he said.

"Kelly has breakfast on still, if you want to eat before you go. I'll just text her." He pulled his phone out of his back pocket and looked at Boone, waiting.

"I never say no to breakfast," Boone said, thinking of how he'd fed his to his dogs. "Especially when your wife's cooking." He grinned and stepped toward the barn. "So what am I doing out today? Pete said he's got something I need to see?"

Squire finished his text and followed Boone into the barn. "One of Pete's best therapy horses is sick," he said.

"Or something. I can't quite make sense of it, and Pete suggested I call you."

"Why's that?" Boone headed toward the cluster of men down at the other end of the barn.

"Because he thinks you're a better vet than I am."

Boone chuckled and shook his head. "That's not true." He suspected he knew why Pete had suggested him, but he didn't press Squire to say it out loud. After all, Boone didn't want to be reminded of the hundreds of cattle he hadn't been able to save on a ranch outside of San Antonio.

"What've we got?" Boone joined the circle when the other cowboys and ranch hands made room for him. He recognized Ethan, his wife, Brynn, Cal—also a vet—Pete, and Bennett. A few others loitered too, but Boone couldn't remember all of their names.

His gaze migrated to the horse in the pen, and his heartbeat bumped over itself. "It's Peony?" He pushed forward to the rails and went over them. "Why didn't you say it was Peony?"

He didn't wait for Pete to answer. There wasn't anything to say anyway. But Boone loved this gentle, cream-colored horse. She'd rescued a lot of people, from veterans with physical limitations, to children with mental disabilities, to men like Boone who just felt broken inside.

Stroking the horse down her nose, he said, "Someone tell me what's going on with her."

Cal said, "She's tender in the abdomen. Dehydrated. Lethargic."

"Stool?"

"None." Pete joined Cal at the fence. "She's been like this for about a day."

Boone's brain spun, trying to find something that would cause these pretty common symptoms. "Constipation." He ran his hands down Peony's neck, not feeling anything abnormal.

She lay perfectly still while he touched her back, but as soon as he moved his hands to her belly, she tensed and nickered at him, a clear warning not to touch her.

He checked her hooves, seeing nothing out of the ordinary, and gingerly trailed his fingers up her front legs. "She's swollen here." He stood and faced the group. "What's she been eating?"

An idea formed in his mind, but he needed to examine things from all sides. Think through all possibilities first. He wouldn't rush a diagnosis again.

"Nothing out of the ordinary," Pete said.

A silver-haired man joined the group. "Oh, Boone's here. Good," Garth said. "Where are we?"

"He's asking about her diet. It hasn't changed." Pete wore the concern plainly in his blue eyes.

"Didn't she go out with that new group a couple of days ago?" Garth glanced around, meeting Squire's eye and then Pete's.

"What group?" Squire asked.

"Our new working horses," he said.

"She went," Ethan said. "No one rode her. We just took her to have her calm spirit help the yearlings."

"So?" Pete asked, looking at Boone and then Garth.

"Where did they go?" Boone asked, focusing on Ethan now. "What did they eat out there?" Boone studied Peony again and went back over the fence. "Show me."

"It's hours out there," Ethan said, looking at Garth. "We went out to sector ten. There's a stream out there. Some trees. Grass."

"What kind of trees?"

Ethan's face blanked. "I have no idea."

Boone turned to Squire. "How fast can I get there in an ATV?" Desperation coiled in Boone. He couldn't lose Peony, because he needed her for his therapy session next weekend.

Forty minutes later, Ethan pointed slightly to the right, and Squire adjusted the side-by-side toward the smear of trees in the distance. Garth rode beside Boone in the backseat, and the tension between the four men hadn't lessened at all.

Once Squire brought the ATV to a stop, Boone jumped out and started searching the ground. Nothing looked toxic. No bright yellow flowers in any direction, which could indicate ragwort.

After a few more feet, though, Boone stepped on something hiding in the long grass. A crunch sounded under his boot, and he lifted his foot and felt around until he came up with the broken shell of an acorn.

"She's eaten acorns," he said, motioning the other men over. He looked up, the brim of his cowboy hat preventing him from examining the trees too closely. "Are these oaks?"

He stood, noting more acorns—dried from last autumn —on the ground. Sure enough, four large oaks stood among the rest of the trees thriving along this little stream.

"Oak leaves, acorns, and branches can poison a horse." He spun and headed back to the ATV. "Let's get back and get her on an IV. I'll administer an activated charcoal dose as well, and then all we can do is hope for the best."

They returned to the ranch, and Boone went about administering to Peony while Squire and Ethan filled everyone else in. He listened to Squire give instructions for the oak clean-up as well, and admiration for the man pulled through Boone. He was also very, very good at running a ranch and inspiring his men.

Once Boone finished, he joined everyone else as they headed over to the homestead for a late breakfast.

"Thank you." Pete's relief wasn't hard to find on his face as they walked side-by-side. "Sorry to pull you from church."

"Oh, it's nothing." Boone waved his hand. It was nothing because he didn't go to church. He wasn't sure why Pete thought he did. Boone's family was in the ultra-religious category, but he'd stopped going in college. One more way to rebel against the family legacy, he supposed. It wasn't that he didn't believe in God. Simply that he couldn't be bothered with one more thing to do. And the fact that his non-existent Sabbath worship didn't satisfy his father appealed to him too.

His phone chimed, and he let the others go ahead of him up the steps as he checked it. His mother had said, *Just saying hi. Love you!*

The door leading to the kitchen above closed, leaving Boone in the quiet countryside, the blue sky above him whispering that there was a higher power on this earth, and it had just helped him save a horse's life.

Pride and accomplishment puffed out Boone's chest. His father didn't understand why he couldn't take care of pets closer to home, but Boone argued that Three Rivers wasn't that far from Hill Country. He could be home within hours if there was an emergency.

A sense of...rightness descended on him. He wasn't sure how to classify it. Comfort? Peace?

No, gratitude.

Boone was grateful for the chance he'd had to go to school, earn his degree, and have a career he enjoyed. He checked his watch and wondered what time church started and if he could show up smelling like charcoal and horse.

Love you too, Mom, he texted back and headed up the steps to join his ranch friends. If one of them went to church, Boone would think about going too.

Chapter Four

"Here you go, Mama." Nicole had never been a mother, but she extended the spoonful of oatmeal toward her mom, who stared straight ahead, just like she would a baby. Her hair needed to be washed, but Nicole didn't have time before church. She didn't like being late, and no one would come visit until tomorrow anyway.

Mama opened her mouth and ate the oatmeal Nicole had spiked with honey and brown sugar to get her to eat it easier. "Daddy?" she called over her shoulder.

Her father's chair creaked in the kitchen and he appeared a few moments later. He pushed his glasses up onto his head, which bore thick, white hair.

"Are you coming to church?"

"Just for a few minutes," he said. "I don't like to leave Mama for more than about a half-hour."

"So we'll drive separately." Sometimes her father came, and sometimes he didn't. Nicole had secretly been hoping to go to church alone today, if only so that if Boone showed up, he wouldn't see her still attached to her parents.

Not that Boone had ever shown up. And she and him hadn't exactly been on friendly enough terms to discuss their religious beliefs. Maybe he went to church somewhere else. It wasn't like the little church she attended was the only one in town, though Pastor Scott was the best.

Nicole liked his youthful sermons, his jovial personality, his way of looking at problems like they were opportunities. So many of his sermons had encouraged her to go for a promotion at the animal clinic, and she'd worked her way from a high school volunteer to the office administrator over the years.

Of course, she'd never been able to turn her family situation into an opportunity, but she had managed to find her own place and move out a few years ago. She finished feeding her mother and washed up in the kitchen with lemon-smelling soap before dropping a kiss on her father's forehead and saying, "I'll see you over there."

Nicole liked to arrive at church early, let the serene atmosphere infuse her soul, listen to the notes of the organ filter out of the open doors and into the air around her. She took a deep, deep breath and felt at home.

She glanced around, her love for her hometown real and large. She'd never wanted to leave Three Rivers, not really. She had wanted to be a veterinarian, but then Mama got sick and Nicole hadn't been able to leave to go to college. She couldn't. Wouldn't.

She'd thought Dr. Von would train her to be the one who could tend to the cats, dogs, birds, and guinea pigs the residents brought into the clinic. He'd started to teach her about different drugs and how to use the x-ray machines. She'd even administered a few vaccinations before Dr. Von got sick. Then he'd left the clinic, and it looked like the whole thing would have to close if someone didn't buy it and hire a new veterinarian.

Nicole had wanted to buy Puppy Pawz so badly. No one knew the ins and outs of it better than she did. But she simply didn't have the money—and she'd wondered if she could handle her aging parents and an animal shelter and hospital at the same time.

In the end, it hadn't mattered. Boone Carver had shown up, and he'd bought the clinic.

Nicole felt sideswiped. One day she was giving a great Dane his deworming shot and the next tall, handsome, powerful Boone walked through the door with his white lab coat, impressive muscles, and impossible handwriting. She seriously couldn't even read half of what Boone wrote, and most of the time it wasn't her fault. Sometimes—*one* time—she'd been impossible on purpose.

Nicole entered the church and took her seat on the third row in the chapel, leaving a space on the end for her father. The pulpit sat below a beautiful stained glass window depicting the Savior delivering his Sermon on the Mount. She gazed up at it, the sunlight streaming through the multi-colored pieces and throwing light across the stage holding the pulpit.

Nicole smiled, enjoying the music as other patrons started arriving. She closed her eyes and breathed in the peace she felt here. *Help me get over Boone's intrusion*, she prayed. She'd never admitted that he hadn't pranced into town with the sole purpose of ruining her life. It had been easier to dislike him if she believed he'd done exactly that.

Though she hadn't spent much time with him outside of work, she'd seen enough of a glimpse into the man's life to know he wasn't the monster she'd imagined.

And she needed to let go of that image, because he seemed like a guy she'd be interested in getting to know better. No one in town had caught her eye, and she didn't want to let maybe her only chance slip away because she was too unwilling to forgive.

She half-expected the negative feelings she'd harbored, cultivated, and encouraged for a year to magically dissipate. When they didn't, she sighed and added, *I'll look for the good in him. Just show it to me*, to her prayer.

Daddy slid onto the bench beside her just moments before Pastor Scott got up and began the sermon. Nicole wasn't sure why, but she turned and scanned the chapel for Boone. She didn't see him, of course. She hadn't truly expected to.

Her attention wandered during the sermon, mostly because she was still searching for a way to get the relief she needed. Finally, about the time her father slipped away and back to Mama, Nicole realized she'd have to talk to Boone and...well, talk to Boone. Maybe tell him why she'd been Miss McNasty Pants for a whole year.

He'd already said he'd find out why she didn't like him. As Nicole mouthed along with the closing song—she never sang in public due to her extreme stage fright—she realized the reason she'd been so cold with him was because she *did* like him. Her frowns, her folded arms, her complete exasperation with his work were all defenses against liking him.

She shot to her feet with the epiphany and stepped into the aisle, intending to find Boone and talk to him right now. She'd go to his house if she had to.

She slammed into a hard body, and stumbled. "Oh. Sorry." Pain started in her cheekbone, which had collided with—Boone's collarbone. "Boone—"

"Hey, you okay?" He reached out and touched her arm, sending a string of sparks down to her fingertips and straight into her chest.

Nicole gasped. Concern crossed Boone's face. "Did I hurt you? I just saw you sitting down in the front, and I came back to see if you wanted to...." He trailed off when he realized he still had his hand on her arm. He stared at the point of contact and snatched his hand back like her skin had caught fire.

She'd never felt such fireworks before, and she craved the razzle, snazzle, pop of that heat in her bloodstream again. She could barely swallow. And speaking? Not happening at the moment.

Thankfully, Boone seemed as equally mute. His dark eyes searched hers, and she saw so much swimming in their depths—longing, passion, desire.

Nicole almost scoffed. He wasn't pining after her. Was he? Could he?

She brushed her bangs out of her eyes and did something she'd never done before. "What are you doing for lunch today?" she asked.

An hour later, Nicole had changed from her boring navy church dress into a more summery, flowery sundress. She wore a pair of sandals with thin straps and carried Valcor in a little purse on her elbow.

Boone had agreed to meet her at Riverwalk Park instead of the dog park where they'd met yesterday. There were a dozen picnic tables along the river. They were usually full on Sunday afternoons, but Nicole had been praying for a solid hour that there would be one open, because Boone said his dogs loved to swim.

She rounded a bend in the walking path, hoping the picnic table just ahead would be empty. Her heart sank when she found someone sitting there, then rebounded when that person stood and lifted his arm, calling, "Nicole."

A grin split her face and she tried to tame it before he

got close enough to see it. "Boone." He wore a pair of jeans, a gray T-shirt with a ninja on it, and a black cowboy hat. He'd never worn his hat in the office, but he did go out to Three Rivers Ranch twice a week, and she imagined him out there, rugged, wild, and gorgeous.

"You look nice." He met her on the lawn and took the picnic basket she carried.

She had no idea how to respond to a compliment from someone like him. No one paid her compliments, and she wasn't exactly the type of woman who should be getting them anyway.

She missed a step, sure most women who regularly received compliments like "You look nice," would probably say something like, "So do you," or "Thank you," and then duck their head flirtatiously.

Nicole said, "I made ham and Muenster sandwiches," and cleared her throat. "And there's some turkey and Swiss too. And I brought grapes, and baby carrots, and lots of dog treats." She couldn't get her voice to stop, and Boone tossed her a healthy smile.

"Sounds great." He set the food on the table and took his position on the bench again. She rounded the table and set Valcor on the end of it farthest from them.

"Should we let the dogs go?"

"After we eat," he said. "I need to be able to keep my eye on Leia." He gave her a mischievous look. "She tends to get in trouble off-leash."

"You should put her on a lead line."

"I brought one."

Of course he did, and somehow the fact that the man had thought of everything didn't annoy her the way it normally would. Fine, maybe it did a little.

He lifted sandwiches out of the basket. "Can I have one of each?"

"How far did you run this morning?"

"I didn't run this morning," he said. "I went out to Three Rivers and helped a horse. Breakfast was cold by the time we finished."

"How much do you usually run on Sundays?"

"Depends on the Sunday," he said. "Today I should've done five miles."

"I guess you can have two sandwiches then." She smiled and pulled the baby carrots toward her. "I can't even imagine *walking* five miles."

"I like to run."

She pulled a ham sandwich toward her. "It's a different look than the cowboy hat." She raised her right eyebrow, which elicited a laugh from him.

"I've always wished I could do that." He beamed at her again and flicked his cowboy hat. "This is a relic from my childhood. My family owns a cattle ranch."

"So you're a real live cowboy?" Nicole wished this news didn't accelerate her heartbeat, but it did. She lived in Texas, after all.

He chuckled. "Not for a few years now."

"You work out at Three Rivers." She seemed to be

doing okay at this flirting thing. "You don't wear the hat out there?"

He ducked his chin, the cowboy hat coming between them. A chuckle came out of his mouth, and Nicole met his smile with one of her own when their eyes met again.

Electricity flowed back and forth between them, and Nicole liked the sizzle of it. "Do you miss it? The ranch?"

"No," he said pretty quickly. "I know I'm doing what I'm supposed to be doing. I like working with animals. Besides, I still get to go out to a ranch." His chuckle this time was nervous and slightly shaky. "Sometimes I get along better with dogs and horses than people." He looked at her and glanced away quickly.

"I know what you mean," Nicole muttered, determined to end her not-dating streak. "Is this a date?" she blurted.

Boone stopped chewing, his sandwich frozen halfway to his mouth. He blinked a couple of times, those beautiful eyes drinking up hers. He swallowed. "A date?" he repeated. He set his sandwich down. "Do you want it to be a date?"

Nicole had completely lost her senses, because she found herself nodding.

"Then it's a date," he said with a grin, leaning toward her with an edge in his eyes that sent excitement racing through her whole body.

Chapter Five

Boone liked it when Nicole looked at him with that teasing sparkle in her hazel eyes, when she laughed at something he'd said, when she asked questions about his real life. He liked that he'd worn his cowboy hat so he could push it low on his forehead and sneak glances at Nicole and she wouldn't know he was looking.

He wasn't sure what had turned her from cold to hot, but he wasn't sorry about it. Just like he hadn't been sorry he'd darkened the door of the church where Squire went. He hadn't arrived in time to catch the pastor's name, but he'd learned that he was Kelly's cousin's husband and that he said really good things.

Nicole finished eating and she packed up the picnic basket while Boone enjoyed the Sabbath Day sunshine. "You want to walk the dogs a bit?" he asked.

"You're the one with the big dogs." She picked up the

doggie purse which itty bitty Valcor hadn't attempted to get out of. "But I could walk." She flashed him one of those sultry smiles he could get used to, and stood up.

He unlooped the leashes from the table bench and picked up the picnic basket. He left it on the edge of the grass next to a bush. "We can get this when we come back."

Nicole didn't say anything, just stepped with her dog. Boone's bare arms soaked up the sunshine and he let Vader and Leia off their leashes. Vader yelped and Leia sprinted for the creek. He laughed as they splashed into the water, their faces so full of joy and wild abandon.

"Does Taz swim?"

"He thinks he can." She bent and loosed his leash, freeing the little dog. He ran toward the creek but came up short of entering it. He barked at the two dogs swimming away from him. "See?" Nicole laughed and Boone enjoyed the look of happiness on her face. He rarely saw it, and he wanted to be the reason she smiled and laughed like that.

"They'll keep up." Boone nodded toward the path and Nicole stepped with him. His fingers flexed and curled, curled and flexed. They itched to touch hers, but literally forty-eight hours ago, he'd left work frustrated with the woman because she'd ignored his perfect paperwork.

Every emotion Boone had ever felt warred inside. He felt sure his brain would explode from all the thinking, the rethinking, the speculating, the circling back. Nicole stepped and he stepped, and their fingers brushed.

Pure adrenaline surged through him and on the next step, he fixed his hand in hers. He glanced at her out of the corner of his eye, trying to judge her reaction. Her fingers felt a bit stiff in his, but it had been a while since he'd held hands with a woman.

Her dress billowed in the slight breeze, as did her yellow hair that she'd only pinned back on the sides today. She'd had it braided at church, but she'd undone it and it flowed over her shoulders in pretty waves.

"Tell me about your family," he said. "Brothers? Sisters?"

"Two older brothers and an older sister. They live all over the place. My oldest brother actually practices law in Grand Cayman."

Boone whistled. "Wow. You ever go visit?"

Nicole shook her head, and her sadness scented the air. "My mother is ill."

He mentally kicked himself. He'd known that. Joanne had told him in the first couple of weeks he'd come to Three Rivers. He'd just forgotten.

"That's right. I'm sorry." He squeezed her hand. "What does she have?"

"Dementia started a few years ago. I managed to move out before she forgot who I was. I still go over and take care of her and Daddy almost every night."

Boone wished he had a way to make everything in Nicole's life okay. But he couldn't do that. Only God could, and often God didn't. But one thing his parents had taught him was that God often put the right people in our lives, at the right time, to provide exactly what we needed.

Maybe God had allowed Boone to make peace with Nicole because she needed it. Perhaps *he* needed *her*.

"She was diagnosed with ovarian cancer last year," Nicole continued. "She refused treatment, so we're just...." She swallowed.

"It's okay," Boone whispered. He tugged Nicole closer and squeezed her hand. "I have an older brother and a younger sister. Middle child syndrome here." He kept talking about where he'd grown up, the chores he'd hated, the horses he'd loved, and why he decided to become a veterinarian.

Nicole seemed content to just let him talk, and they made it around the park and back to the picnic basket. "Thanks, Boone," she said, retrieving her belongings. "I have to go."

"Oh yeah?" He bent to leash his dogs, glad the sun was so warm and hot today so they were mostly dry after their earlier swim.

She tucked her hair behind her ear. "Yeah, I help deliver meals on Sunday evenings for shut-ins."

Surprise shot through Boone. "You do?"

"Every week." She met his eye. "I find that I don't feel so...." She sighed. "I don't know. I feel better when I'm helping other people."

Boone had a feeling she knew exactly how she felt and simply didn't want to say it. And that the service she rendered on Sunday evenings alleviated those feelings. He cocked his head and chose to ignore her evasion. "That's how I feel about helping animals."

She grinned at him, and he leaned down and ran his lips across her cheek. "See you Tuesday? Or maybe you'd like to, I don't know, go to breakfast tomorrow before I head out to the ranch?"

Nicole reached up and touched her cheek where his lips had been. "I eat breakfast," she said as if she'd never said those words in that order before.

"The pancake house?" he asked. "I can come pick you up if you want."

"I'll meet you there."

"Great." Boone grinned at her, and he couldn't stop.

WHEN HE GOT HOME, he found a shiny white truck sitting in his driveway. Lord Vader recognized it and whined, leaping over Leia to the open window and back to Boone, who laughed.

"Yeah, Dylan's here." He pulled in beside his friend's truck and got out, nearly tripping over Lord Vader as the dog leapt from the vehicle and tore into the garage. His tail wagged and slobber dripped from his mouth as he waited eagerly at the entrance to the house.

Boone opened the door and said, "Vader incoming," before letting the dog in. Leia followed, and Dylan's laughter and high-pitched warblings to the dogs came next.

"What are you doin' here?" Boone smiled as he entered his kitchen. He clapped the first friend he'd made in Three Rivers on the back. "I hope you didn't expect me to cook."

Dylan scoffed. "I know better than that."

"So you brought something?" Boone looked around for pizza boxes and found nothing.

"My mom sent leftovers. Check the fridge." He slapped a copy of the town's newspaper on the counter. "Have you seen this?"

Boone barely glanced at the paper, the letters swimming into formations that made no sense, before turning to the fridge. "What's that?"

"There's an article about the animal clinic."

Boone found a few plastic containers with chicken cordon bleu and twice baked potatoes and Dylan's mother's special spinach salad. "I am texting your mother thank you right now." He sent the text, grateful Meredith Walker took such good care of him. "And what does the article say?"

"Read it." Dylan nudged it a little closer.

A blip of panic radiated through Boone. He'd done an exceptional job of hiding his reading disability, and he'd worked harder than anyone to finish his education and get his degree. No one knew how hard it was to read charts at work or file the proper paperwork. Exhaustion engulfed him just thinking about it.

He picked up the paper anyway and scanned the biggest, boldest letters. They weren't about Puppy Pawz. He finally found what he was looking for when Dylan pointed to the bottom right corner. E's flipped themselves over and L's and I's switched places.

He squinted, his brain making up for the discrepancies his eyes sent it. "Our building does need to be updated," he said. "The air conditioning is fickle. Who wrote this?" He found Gentry Pace's name on the article, and his heart sank. "I wonder who she talked to." He managed to keep the concern out of his voice.

Though he and Gentry had gone out a few times before calling it quits, everything in the article was correct, and he hoped her appeal to the city would land on ears willing to hear. There were several buildings around town that could use some updating, and Puppy Pawz happened to be housed in one of them.

He put the paper down. "That was a good article. Do you know Gentry Pace?"

"Not super well. She's been here a few years, running a flower shop and writing for the paper."

"I went out with her a few times." He stuck the potatoes and chicken in the microwave and started it.

"Do you think that's why she wrote this?"

"It's not bad, Dylan. I hope the city does something."

"So how was your date?" Dylan could jump from topic to topic faster than anyone Boone had ever known.

Boone grinned. "It was fantastic."

"I thought Nicole Hymas didn't like you."

Boone's euphoria slipped a little. "I didn't think she did. I think she's probably still trying to figure out if she does or not." And he still needed to figure out why she'd given him the cold shoulder for so long.

"You've always liked a challenge."

Boone let his comment slide. So he was a bit on the competitive side. Didn't mean he was only interested in Nicole for the chase. If that were true, he'd have been shamelessly flirting with her for the past twelve months and eight days regardless of her hostility.

"Does she have any friends?" Dylan asked.

"I thought you were dating the receptionist in the mayor's office." Boone popped the top on the salad container and got a noseful of mustard and olive oil.

"That didn't work out." He shrugged. "She said she's not interested in an electrician. I told her we were *electrifying*." He grinned as if the break up didn't faze him. "She said she thought of me as her brother."

"Ouch," Boone said. "There's a receptionist at the animal clinic."

"Yeah, Joanne Bailey." Dylan's tone didn't convey excitement.

"You know her?"

"Dated her in high school."

Boone chuckled. He should've known. Dylan had grown up in this small town, and he knew everyone in it.

"Well, you already know everyone who's available then. Doesn't matter who Nicole's friends are."

"I guess not." Dylan exhaled and said, "So who's playing tonight?"

"I think the Rangers are at the Rockies." Boone took his food into the living room and sat on the other end of the couch from Dylan, who flipped through the channels until he found the baseball game.

Boone relaxed, all the things that had been keeping him awake in the past week gone. With the memory of Nicole's hand still in his, he enjoyed the secret of their walk in the park and their upcoming date in the morning.

And he'd never been happier animals couldn't talk, because Vader and Leia sure had cuddled up to Dylan and would probably tell him anything.

The traitors.

The doorbell rang, and someone knocked, and he looked at Dylan and then the door like he wasn't sure what to do.

But no one came over on Sunday evenings, except the person who was already here. So who was at the door?

Chapter Six

Nicole showed up at the soup kitchen on the south side of Three Rivers, almost ten minutes late. And she was never late, a fact that Alice Sweet pointed out to her with a cocked eyebrow.

"I know," Nicole said. "I just lost track of time." So maybe she'd sank into her couch after her park date—a *real* date—with Boone.

She hung her purse on a hook just inside the door and pulled her hair into a ponytail. She exhaled and clapped her hands. "Okay, where am I tonight?"

"Boxing." Alice pointed past all the meal prep and sectioning, and toward the end of the line of volunteers. "And I want to hear about the reason you were late." Her green eyes shone with excitement and knowledge, and Nicole gave her a smile.

"You already know."

"It's a small town." Alice shrugged. "And you never date."

"Not never."

"Name the last man you went out with."

"So I'm on boxing?" Nicole started walking away, not wanting to get into the reasons she hadn't been out with anyone in a while. She'd been so focused on getting the credentials she needed to run the veterinary clinic, and then when the prospect of buying it had come up, she'd spent a few months researching that.

And then there was Mama.... No, Nicole didn't have time to date. It wasn't that she didn't want to. At least that was what she'd been telling herself as another day, another week, another month went by where she spent all of her time at Puppy Pawz or with her ailing and aging parents.

She joined the crew sliding the meals into plastic bags to be vacuumed sealed and passed them down the row to the two guys putting the sealed trays into boxes.

She enjoyed her work in the soup kitchen, and she chatted with the people around her. Sundays saw more volunteers than other days of the week, Nicole included, but she didn't have the energy or stamina to put in a full day of work at the clinic, check on her parents, and then come to the kitchen too.

The Sabbath was her day of rest, the day she rejuvenated herself, prepped herself mentally and spiritually for the week ahead.

This week, she hadn't felt as thrashed as she normally

did. Not nearly as annoyed. So maybe starting a little friendship with Boone Carver wasn't such a bad idea.

But as she stacked the meals she'd be responsible for delivering, she knew she was interested in more than friendship with the tall cowboy-slash-veterinarian.

Is that so bad? she asked herself as she helped Alice go over the checklist to make sure everyone in Three Rivers got their meal tonight.

She didn't think so.

"We have fifteen extra," Alice said, looking up and glancing around. "Ellen. Craig. Everyone come get a meal for tonight." She looked at Nicole. "Take one or two. No reason for this to go to waste."

She thought of her parents as the others who hadn't left yet came over and took meals. There were still seven left, and she asked, "Can I take one for my parents too?"

"Of course." Alice made another check on her clipboard. "Take what you want." She turned away as Craig asked her a question, and Nicole snagged four meals.

It would take her a couple of hours to deliver the dozens of meals she had already stacked in her car, but her parents would be okay until then. Mama would probably be asleep anyway, and she could eat the pork chop and mashed potatoes for lunch tomorrow.

Nicole looked at the two meals in her left hand, wondering what time Boone ate and if he liked applesauce with his proteins.

With the window down, Nicole enjoyed the serene

feel of Three Rivers. People populated the parks and Main Street, but the residential areas of town were draped in silence and contentment.

And that was why Nicole loved doing the deliveries on Sunday night, even in the winter months when the sun sank sooner and she didn't finish until darkness had fallen.

Doing this, she could feel the warmth of God, almost like He was smiling down on her as she did the simple, small service for those who just needed a hot meal.

A COUPLE OF HOURS LATER, she only had the four meals on the front seat left. Hers, her parents', and Boone's. She knew where he lived, as she ran the clinic he bought. She knew all kinds of personal information about him, but she was a professional through and through.

So she would not simply drive to his house and show up with a lame sealed dinner he probably didn't need. The man clearly had some money, and not only because he owned the animal hospital and shelter.

He'd bought and moved into one of the big, new houses on the north end of town, and Nicole had seen the price tag on those as she'd looked at them too.

She decided to stop by her parents' house first, and she knocked at the same time she entered the house. Sure enough, Mama was asleep in the recliner in the front room, and Nicole tiptoed past her and into the kitchen.

"Hey, Daddy. I brought food." Her father sat at the kitchen table, the radio playing as he did a crossword puzzle.

"Hey, sweetie. What is it tonight?"

"Pork and applesauce, with potatoes and green beans." She handed him one of the boxes. "Sixty seconds in the microwave," she reminded him. "Maybe Mama can eat the applesauce and potatoes for lunch tomorrow."

He beamed up at her. "She'll love them." He stood and accepted the boxes, putting one in the refrigerator and opening the second one. He poked holes in the plastic along the top and stuck it in the microwave.

"How's work?" he asked.

"Great." Nicole smiled at him as the food rotated around and around. She might have complained about the clinic—and Boone—in the past when there was leftover food and she brought some to her parents.

But tonight, she just grinned and said, "I have one more stop to make, Daddy. See you tomorrow." She gave him a kiss on the cheek and went back to her car.

She sat with her hands at ten and two, her options swimming through her mind.

Nicole felt like she was slowly going crazy. She had never once considered driving Boone's house—at least not without a few dozen eggs in her arsenal.

A twinge of guilt pulled through her, and she eased out of her parents' driveway. Maybe she'd just drive around, see where the car took her.

She had a full tank of gas, and the closer she radiated to the north edge of town, the tighter she gripped the steering wheel.

She finally took the turn to go out to Three Rivers Ranch, the last of the day's light starting to turn golden and gray at the same time.

The new subdivision was up on the left, and Nicole felt a blazing rush of bravery as she took the turn. Boone lived in the house at the end of the street, and a big white truck already sat in the driveway with his black one.

Another car was parked on the curb, and as she eased to a stop behind it, Boone's front door opened.

A woman stepped outside, but she didn't look happy. With the window down, Nicole could hear the conversation whether she wanted to or not, and she very clearly heard Boone say, "Just go on home, Ellie."

The blonde came down the stairs, a scowl on her face. She didn't cut across the grass, but her four-inch heels didn't really allow for that kind of walking anyway.

She glared at Nicole as she fumbled to open her car. "Hope you're not here for either one of them. They're so arrogant." She yanked open the door, got behind the wheel, and drove away in a roar.

Nicole watched her go, her heart thumping against the back of her throat.

"What are you doing' here?" Boone's decidedly deep and male voice had Nicole spinning back around.

He practically leaned through her passenger window,

somehow bending his tall body almost in half to do so. He wore a smile the size of Texas itself and opened the car door as if he'd get in.

Which he did.

"Oh, I—" She grabbed the boxes of food, one of which she'd brought him, before he could smash them and positioned them on her lap instead.

With him in the car, even with the windows down, the space seemed impossibly small. Maybe it was just because his shoulders were so big. Or because his cologne hit every note she wanted in her pheromones.

She turned back toward her own window and tried to get a breath of air that wasn't scented or filled with Boone. "Remember how I said I deliver meals on Sunday?" She faced him again, and lifted the boxes slightly. "There were extra tonight, and I wondered if you wanted one."

He watched her with those intoxicating eyes, and the sparkle in them increased by the moment. "What makes you think I can't feed myself?"

"Maybe because you eat out every day for lunch?"

He laughed, the sound absolutely delicious. Nicole reached out and traced her fingertips along his ear and into his hair.

He silenced, and she stared at him, sure she'd lost her mind.

She pulled her hand back as if he'd electrocuted her. "Sorry."

He looked a bit on the pale side, and his face had gone so blank.

"It's just pork and potatoes," she said, thrusting one of the boxes at him. She really wanted to know if he liked fruit with his pork, but she wasn't going to impose herself on him when he'd already kicked out one blonde woman.

He took the box, some of the shock melting from his rugged features. "Who's that one for?"

"Me."

"You want to come in and eat with me?"

She shook her head, a laugh coming out of her mouth she didn't recognize. She couldn't remember the last time she had something to laugh about. "No, I saw how blonde women leave your place."

He reached over and slipped his fingers through hers, a chuckle vibrating his chest. "That was Dylan's ex-girlfriend. I guess she went to his place and didn't find him there, so she came here."

"Dylan Walker?"

Boone shot her a glance. "Yeah. You know him?"

"Of course. He grew up here, same as me."

"Oh, right." Boone still looked apprehensive, and Nicole gave him a small smile.

"I like him fine, if you're worried about that," she said.

His features relaxed and softened then, and he said, "You sure you don't want to come in?"

"With you and Dylan? I think I'll pass."

"Your loss," he said. "We've got baseball on in there and it's a lot cooler than out here."

"You're not charming me with the baseball." Nicole giggled again, and acted without thinking for the second or third time that night.

She leaned over and swept her lips across his cheek. "I'll see you in the morning, okay?"

He took the cue and got out of the car, leaning back in through the window to say, "Okay. Thanks for the food. You're right. I don't really know how to feed myself, so this is great."

She laughed again, the gesture so freeing she finally believed the saying that laughter was the best medicine. Easing the car away from the curb, she couldn't resist checking her rearview mirror to watch Boone walk back inside his house.

But he wasn't walking away from her. He stood on the sidewalk and watched her drive away, a ridiculous smile on his face.

Which caused an equally ludicrous smile to appear on Nicole's face too.

Definitely more than friendship, her brain screamed at her as she drove out of his subdivision and on back to her own house. As she pulled into the driveway of her much older home, she thanked the Lord for her little patch in Three Rivers and for a few stolen minutes with Boone Carver.

Chapter Seven

Boone watched the sun rise as Lord Vader and Princess Leia ran with the other ranch dogs. He spent his Mondays and Wednesdays out at Three Rivers with the dogs, cats, chickens, calves, horses, bulls, and cattle on the ranch, and they were two of the best days of his week.

Impatience seethed just beneath his skin this morning, though. Because one of the main reasons he'd enjoyed his time out at the ranch was because it meant he wasn't stuck at the animal hospital with a dictator of an office administrator.

But now that Nicole was acting nicer.... Boone found himself wanting to leave the ranch and get into town as soon as possible.

"Mornin'," Garth Ahlstrom, the foreman of the ranch,

said as he passed. A young boy followed behind him, and he glanced up at Boone from under his hat too.

"Mornin', Boone," the boy said in much the same tone as his father.

"Hey, Jake. Where you guys off to this morning?"

"I don't know."

"Bullpen," Garth called over his shoulder. "Re-runging."

That didn't sound like a job Boone would want to do—and exactly the reason he'd left his family's ranch in Grape Seed Falls—and the boy's non-enthusiasm for his morning task made a lot of sense to Boone.

He still couldn't help a chuckle as the boy continued to trudge after his father. At least he was obedient and learning to work.

He did love the country stillness. The way the sun took it's time giving light to Texas, as if He wanted to breathe life into the best state in the Union one slow moment at a time.

Boone did enjoy the way he could feel peace when on a ranch. They really were special places, and Three Rivers Ranch functioned as a community almost by itself. Dozens of people lived and worked out here, a good forty minutes from town and the nearest grocery store.

"You ready?" Cal stepped up beside Boone and put his boot on the bottom rung of the fence where Boone was watching the dogs still running through the fields.

"Yes, sir," Boone said, the way he would've to his

father. "I'm headed into town for a breakfast," he added. "Just for a couple of hours. I'll be back by ten, and I won't fall behind in the work."

Cal laughed, as if Boone had said something funny. "I don't care what you do," he said. "Squire doesn't either. Brynn might, as you're supposed to be in her barns today, but whatever." He shrugged and lifted a coffee mug to his lips.

He glanced toward the homestead, but neither of them saw Squire. The three of them always met on Monday mornings, at least for a few minutes, just to get caught up on any pressing animal care needs the ranch had.

Squire and Cal both had their veterinary licenses too, and they both lived on-site. Squire split the full-time care with Cal, and did administrative work during the rest of the day. Cal split his time at Courage Reins, Bowman's Breeds, and the main ranch, making sure every horse on the property was as healthy as possible.

"How's Trina?" Boone asked at the same time Cal asked, "Who are you meeting for breakfast?"

Boone waited for Cal to answer, because he wasn't sure he wanted to talk about Nicole just yet. Which was pretty ridiculous, because he'd held her hand in public yesterday, and the only reason everyone at the ranch didn't know about it was because they lived on the ranch.

Another thing to admire, he thought while Cal detailed how Trina was doing now that the morning sickness had subsided and she'd moved into the second trimester of her pregnancy.

"And how's Sabrina doing with the idea of having a new brother or sister?"

"She's excited," Cal said, finishing his coffee. "She wants it to be a girl, of course." He flashed Boone a smile and said, "Here comes the boss."

Sure enough, Squire was making his way toward them, whistling at his own dog to come to his side. Buddy did, and his step-son Finn treated the canine and gave him a healthy scrub as they continued toward them.

"Morning," Squire said, glancing at both Boone and Cal. Boone imagined his older brother Dwayne to be as serious, nowhere near smiling until noon, at least, and the kind of man like Squire who slept in his cowboy hat.

"Honeybee's finally been retired," he said. "And Peony too, though she's making a pretty remarkable recovery, thanks to you, Boone."

"Glad to hear it," Boone said, and he genuinely was. He did love animals, and he wondered why his father had thought that wasn't noble enough.

But his dad had wanted a ranch his whole life, and he and his mother had sacrificed for years to build Grape Seed Falls Ranch into what it was today.

But Dwayne loved the ranch and wanted it and worked it. Boone wouldn't even have a place there anyway, even if he had stayed in Texas Hill Country.

"Everything's humming along real well here," Squire

said next. "So the usual rounds, and Cal's with Courage Reins today, and Boone, you're with Brynn."

"Got it," he said, preparing to give the speech about the breakfast to his cousin.

"He's got a hot date for breakfast," Cal said, elbowing Boone.

"I do not," Boone said, every cell in his body recoiling with the lie. "It's just my office administrator. I don't normally work at the animal hospital on Mondays, but we need to meet. That's all."

Squire watched him for a moment past comfortable. "All right. Just check in with Brynn before you go." He turned, the meeting clearly over.

Cal wandered away with Squire, the two men still talking. Boone let them go, because he needed another moment with just the ranch...and God.

He drew in a deep breath, trying to order the words in his mind to a prayer. It had been a long time since he'd put up a plea to the Lord, but he managed to cobble together a simple sentence.

Help me do what's right.

Whether he meant with his ranch work, his veterinary hospital, or Nicole, he wasn't sure. He needed help with all of it.

BOONE ARRIVED at the pancake house a few minutes before eight and pushed his way inside to find the pastor eating bacon and eggs with the Sheriff. Boone liked to drive really fast, and the cops back home had pulled him over several times. Every time he saw anyone wearing a law enforcement uniform, his stomach turned a bit.

He avoided eye contact with the Sheriff, though his wife had brought in a cat a few months ago and she'd been nice enough. Sandy, the actual owner of the pancake house, smiled at him and said, "Just you?"

He leaned against the counter, a grin flirting with his lips. "Two today."

"Ooh, who are you meeting?" Sandy collected two menus and led him toward a private corner booth.

"You'll see, Miss Nosy." He took the menu and slid into the booth. Sandy laughed and walked away, and Boone caught sight of her husband, Tad, saying something to her as she approached the hostess station again.

Nicole arrived exactly at eight o'clock, and her eyes met his across the distance, but the pastor grabbed her before she could make her way toward him. They spoke for a few minutes, while Nicole tucked her hair and ducked her head and laughed nervously. Whatever the pastor was telling her made her uncomfortable, and Boone wondered what it was.

She wore a pair of jeans and a yellow blouse that made her hair seem whiter than usual. Or maybe that was the fluorescent lighting. She finally made her way to the corner booth and slid in. "Morning."

"What was that about?" He nodded toward the pastor and the Sheriff.

Her defenses flew into place, and her eyes turned cold. "Just some church stuff."

"What kind of church stuff?"

She rolled her eyes. "Pastor Scott wants me to sing in the church choir."

"And you don't want to? You're always walking around the clinic singing or humming."

Horror paraded across her face. "I am not."

He chuckled. "You totally are. Every day."

Her shoulders slumped and she lost the fight in her expression. "Fine. I have stage fright. Are you happy now?"

"No." He reached across the table and took her hands in his. "*Now* I'm happy."

She laughed, a happy little sound that made Boone's pulse skip around inside his chest

"So," he said, enjoying the buzz in his blood he knew belonged to the woman across from him. "Tell me something about you I don't already know."

"Well." She took a deep breath. "I don't think you really know much about me at all."

"I know you're detail-oriented," he said. "And you never miss a deadline. You work hard, and you've never taken a sick day."

She scoffed and picked up her glass of water, removing her fingers from him. They still tingled like he'd been connected to a live wire. "How would you know that? You've been here a year."

"Not everyone in the office has ignored me." Boone regretted the words as soon as they left his mouth. "I mean—"

Sandy arrived at the table and said, "Morning y'all. Coffee?"

"Yes, please," Nicole said, tucking her hair behind her ear, and Boone realized she hadn't pulled it up into her customary bun yet that morning.

He wanted to reach across the table and do the same thing, feel her hair between his fingers.

Once Sandy left, he did reach over and claim her hand again. "I'm sorry," he said. "Want me to tell you something you don't know about me?"

Nicole smiled, though it didn't pack quite the punch it had at the park yesterday. "Yes, let's do that."

Chapter Eight

Nicole floated into the clinic, the memory of Boone's hand in hers hot and strong. Her skin still tingled and everything. She wore a perma-grin that made Joanne cock her head to the side and say, "What happened this weekend?"

Nicole just grinned harder and bypassed the reception desk in favor of her office. She'd eaten breakfast at the pancake house. Everyone in Three Rivers would know by lunchtime. It was impossible to hide things in such a small town.

But for now, the secret was Nicole's—as was that he didn't want his family farm in Hill Country—and she entered her office and closed the door, something she rarely did. A happy sigh escaped her lips as she sat down and tried to focus on what she needed to accomplish that day.

Pet adoption paperwork from last week. The yearly budget, which she'd need Boone to sign off on in the next couple of days. And on days Boone went out to the ranch, she took care of the animal shelter residents alone.

He liked how efficient she was. He liked her hair. He liked her laugh. He wanted to sit by her at church next week. She relived their breakfast, somehow remembering everything he'd said, the sexy way he'd watched her with those dark eyes that he couldn't hide because the cowboy hat was gone.

He had so many sides, he was like a rectangular prism. Turn him this way and he was a veterinarian. That way and he was a marathon runner. Over and he was all cowboy, hiking to remote lakes in Texas Hill Country and fishing, river rafting, and swimming instead of doing the ranch work his father wanted him to. Upside down and he was a normal, well-dressed, good looking man taking a woman to breakfast. Nicole wondered if she could see him again that evening and how to do it without coming across as desperate.

She really could listen to the man talk for hours in that sexy Texan drawl he had. Nicole found herself staring at her dark computer and she jolted. How long had she been daydreaming about Boone? Too long as the clock read just past nine-thirty now. Thirty minutes too long.

She leapt to her feet, determined not to let him dominate her day when he wasn't even in the office. She used to crave the time at Puppy Pawz when he was gone, when the clinic became hers again, when everything went back to how it had been before he showed up.

Now, the vibe at the clinic felt different. It felt... empty. Sterile. She wiped her palms down the front of her scrubs and exited her office.

Joanne stood. "Is it true? You ate breakfast with Boone?"

The gossip had started already. Nicole going into her office first thing on Monday morning and closing the door for over a half-hour had probably sent Joanne into a tizzy. She'd probably sent over a hundred texts, until she'd discovered what had gone down only an hour ago.

Nicole didn't really want to live in denial. A grin graced her face. "I did."

Joanne squealed and glanced around, though the waiting room was vacant. Sure, sometimes an emergency care situation would arise and they'd have to call Boone, but most of the time, the Mondays when he didn't work were quiet and uneventful, with only owners dropping off dogs for daycare.

"Tell me how *that* happened."

The incredulity in Joanne's voice grated against Nicole's nerves, but she supposed the relationship was a bit unconventional. After all, she'd spent every day for the past year glaring at the man. She hadn't exactly been nice to him, and anyone with two eyes had seen it.

She wouldn't have pegged the animal shelter to be a hotbed for gossip, but Joanne did see a lot of people coming in and out of the building. They all interacted with her first, and she had grown up in Three Rivers. She knew everyone and their pets, their parents, their problems. And now she wanted to know what was going on with Nicole and Boone.

Nicole wanted to answer her, but she wasn't sure herself. "Come on rounds with me in the shelter and daycare," she said. Joanne practically fumbled everything on her desk as she reached for the "Be right back. Ring the bell for service" sign and placed it on the counter.

Six years her junior, Joanne had always been nice to Nicole. Nicole, who didn't have a lot of friends because of her work at Puppy Pawz and her constant care of her family. She walked slow, something she never did on the job. She filled the cat food bowls while Joanne washed out water bowls for the dogs.

"We ran into each other at the dog park on Friday morning," Nicole finally said. "It was...strange."

"What does that mean?" Joanne spoke loud to be heard over the running water.

"He seemed different. Less bossy." She thought of him in those tiny running shorts and that shirt made from seemingly space-age material. "More human." Or more god-like, she wasn't sure. Boone wore slacks, a short-sleeved dress shirt in a variety of colors, and a tie to work. He paired his white lab coat with it every single day, making him mature and maddeningly handsome and most definitely out of Nicole's reach.

Joanne didn't say anything, simply moved down the line with fresh water for the canines. The little French bulldog that had come in last week cowered in the corner of her kennel, and Nicole knelt down to look at her. "Hey, Bianca. Come on." The little dog didn't move, and Nicole wondered if she could add a third pet to her household. Valcor would resist, but Taz would be ecstatic to have a dog that actually played with him. Or at least got off the couch.

"What happened?" Joanne paused next to Nicole, who stood and looked her friend in the eyes. Joanne combed her fingers through her red hair and secured it in a ponytail.

"We ran into each other at church," she said, remembering the faint bruise on her cheekbone she'd gotten from *actually* running into him. "Went to the park for a picnic. Then breakfast this morning. Oh, and we met on Saturday at the dog park too."

"A planned meeting?"

"Yes."

Joanne's emerald eyes sparkled like the sun glinting off water. "So you're dating him."

"No—I mean...." Nicole sighed. She'd never really dated anyone before. Before Mama had gotten sick, she'd gone out with a group of friends. She'd interacted with men. But she didn't actually know how to date a man. How to flirt. How to capture the attention of someone as smart and successful as Boone.

"This isn't going to end well, is it?" she asked.

Joanne frowned and moved down the line, collecting the food bowls onto her cart. "Why wouldn't it?"

"For one thing, he lives on the north end of town."

"So what?"

"Those houses up there aren't cheap." And his had been at the end of the street—one of the biggest in the neighborhood.

Joanne scoffed. "That's a non-issue."

"How so?" She thought of her quaint cottage just down the street from the elementary school, in the decidedly older part of town. Sometimes, on a really quiet morning, she could hear the bell ringing. The house itself was nothing spectacular. A couple of small bedrooms. A tiny galley kitchen, and a living room that barely held a full-sized couch. But Nicole hadn't bought the house for the interior. No, all of her passion had been poured into the yard.

"So you think you can't be with him because he has money?" Joanne asked, scooping dog food into clean bowls.

"I don't know," Nicole said. "Maybe because he's my boss. Maybe because I haven't been super nice to him until now." The words poured from her like water through a dam. "Maybe because he's astronomically good looking and I'm just Plain Old Nicole." She took a deep breath to contain the tremors shaking her chest. When had she become weak and self-depreciating?

Sure, she'd been invisible and overlooked her entire life. *An afterthought* ran through her mind. But she'd never been weak. She was the one who stuck around when Mama got sick. She was the one who went to her parents' house every single day to take care of them. She did their dishes and her own. She vacuumed their floor before hers. She'd sacrificed her education, her dreams, her desires, for them.

None of her other siblings had done that, and like a bolt of lightning cutting through the sky, she realized why she'd been so angry with Boone all this time. She was projecting her feelings for her siblings onto him. Their abandonment had become his. Their detachment burned, and she'd taken it out on him.

Joanne set a bowl of dog food in front of Bianca's crate, and the little dog came forward. Nicole scooped her into her arms and patted her soft head. "What do you think, Jo? Do you think I have a chance with Boone?"

"I don't see why not." Joanne faced her, her eyes kind as they usually were. "You're a great catch, Nicole," she said. "I've always thought so."

"I'm ordinary," she said. "Someone like Boone is probably used to *extra*ordinary." She hadn't cared who he'd dated in the past, but again, things like that in Three Rivers were hard *not* to know about.

"Someone like Boone needs someone good, someone grounded, someone who's going to set him straight from time to time."

"I at least do that," Nicole said weakly.

Joanne smiled for half a heartbeat. "You certainly do." It was her way of saying Nicole had been less than kind to Boone. She finished feeding the dogs and wiped down the cart. From the front of the facility, the phone rang. Joanne walked around the kennels to the door. "You're better than you think, Nicole," she said just before she entered the hall and disappeared from sight.

Nicole stayed in the shelter, finished feeding the cats, and talked to Bianca about her issues with herself and Boone. No matter what Joanne said, Nicole knew she was plain. The smattering of freckles across her nose didn't make her special. A million women had that. Her hair was thin, and she scraped it together to make a small bun each day. She wasn't curvy, but she wasn't skinny either.

No, there was absolutely nothing remarkable about her. She knew it; had always known it. She sighed, the euphoria of that morning's breakfast already gone and it wasn't even lunchtime yet.

Chapter Nine

Boone sat in his office, the letters in front of him blurring together into nonsense. It had been a long week, but he and Nicole had fallen into a fantastic rhythm of going to lunch when he was in the office.

Today would be lunch number three, and while he hadn't kissed her yet, he suspected that his fantasies were one of the main reasons he couldn't read the chart for the little dog he was about to perform surgery on.

A simple baby tooth retention that needed to be extracted. But all he could think about was maybe taking Nicole somewhere off Main Street so they could have a more private moment than summer in Three Rivers provided.

Sixteen steps. Sixteen steps and he could ask her what she thought about such an idea.

Not gonna happen, he told himself, blinking and trying

to focus on the dog's weight from that morning. He wasn't due in surgery for another twenty minutes, and he certainly had time to take those sixteen steps and talk to Nicole.

Maybe even kiss her.

Could he kiss her in her office?

It had a door, though since they'd started seeing each other, she'd opened the blinds and left them that way so everyone could see inside.

So her office was out. He'd definitely need to take her somewhere else to get a kiss.

Someone knocked on his doorframe, and he glanced up. "Ready, Doctor?" Joanne stood there, dressed in her scrubs. She'd have everything ready in the operating room, and all Boone would have to do was make sure the little dog got the right amount of medicine and that he took out the right teeth.

"Almost," he said, looking at the chart this time for real and getting his thoughts straight. He couldn't be thinking about Nicole during work.

He had lunch with her.

And he was going to ask her to dinner, soon. A real date. Away from the office. His place. He could order food as well as the next man, and he wanted to see her when she wasn't dressed in scrubs or a skirt suit.

He wanted to see her in her natural environment, maybe snuggle with her on the couch while something played on the TV.

He used to do that with Dylan—minus the snuggling—but he was ready to replace his friend with a woman.

Wasn't he?

He memorized the numbers he needed and headed out of his office and into the operating room. The tiny dog, Rocky, was brought in, and he cradled the yorkie against his chest.

"Hey, bud," he cooed at the dog. "It's gonna be all right now, okay? Let's look at those teeth." He handed the pup back to Joanne, who held him tight while Boone checked on the teeth.

Three of them needed to come out, and none of them were all that loose.

"Four milligrams," he said, covering his hair and stepping over to the sink to wash his hands. Once he was gloved and ready, he set about getting those teeth out.

After the successful surgery, he washed out and went back to his office. He closed the door so he wouldn't dart down the hall to see Nicole.

He'd learned a bit more about her through their casual meals, and he knew her parents were older and her mother was sick. She hadn't detailed too much, and she'd quickly changed the subject to her yard.

Apparently, it was a thing of beauty and had won several awards in Three Rivers over the years. He could just picture her outside, making everything she touched beautiful.

His phone rang and he swiped on the call from Dylan,

which was odd considering it was the middle of the morning.

"What's up?" he asked.

"You up for a weekend on horseback?" he asked.

Boone leaned back in his chair and turned it toward the window. The grass surrounding the building hadn't improved, and it only reminded him how hot it was here.

"I'm surprised you are," he said. "You don't exactly ride horses every day."

"Neither do you," Dylan said.

"A heckuva lot more than you do." In fact, Boone had been on a horse on Wednesday, only two days ago, while he was out at the ranch. He'd had to ride out to a nearby herd and check the hooves on a couple of cows that had found something sharp to step on.

"The community center is short a couple of men for their youth overnight ride, and I thought maybe me and you could go."

"When?" he asked, spinning back to his desk so he could check his schedule, which was scrawled on his desk calendar in Nicole's handwriting.

"We leave in the morning and will be back by noon on Sunday."

"So we'd miss church." Boone didn't see anything on his work calendar that would prevent him from going. He thought through his options. He hadn't been that big of a church-goer for a few years, but he'd felt something out at

Three Rivers after his clumsy prayer, and he sure did want to sit by Nicole in those tiny pews.

"Yeah." Dylan drew the word out. "Do you actually go to church?"

"Yeah, I went last week," he said, the fib falling from his mouth and making him a tad uncomfortable. "Well, I showed up near the end and...yeah. I was thinking about going at the beginning this time."

"Oh, well, if it's a deal-breaker."

"It's not. I can go." If he ended up going, he'd definitely need to see Nicole tonight. Kiss her tonight. "What do I need to do?"

"I'll talk to Jack Marcher and see," Dylan said. "I'll call you back."

"I have another surgery in a few minutes," Boone said. "Leave me a message."

"Deal." Dylan hung up, and Boone reached for the next chart. This was a much bigger dog, here to have bladder stones removed. Boone pushed everything out of his mind—Dylan, horseback riding, and Nicole—and focused.

After all, this was someone's beloved pet, and he wouldn't want his vet to be distracted by a beautiful woman while he operated on Vader or Leia.

He made it through the surgery, which was much more difficult than he'd anticipated. Sometimes they were, when there were no ultrasounds done to know exactly what he'd find once the incisions were made.

But Racer was resting comfortably, and Joanne and Theo would keep an eye on the dogs while he went to lunch. They'd make the calls to the owners when the pups woke up and make sure they were ready to go home.

He could go to lunch and then come back for an easier afternoon of appointments and paperwork. Not that the paperwork was easy. It took him twice as long as other people to get all his Ts crossed and his Is dotted.

But maybe Nicole could help him....

The idea played around in his mind as he made those sixteen steps from his office to hers. "Hey," he said. "You ready for lunch?"

She held up one finger and he realized she was on the phone. He held up both his hands, palms out and backed out of her office.

His stomach growled while he waited, but she came out after only a few minutes, and he marveled at her. How had he missed her sitting right there, all this time?

And why didn't she like him for the first twelve months he'd been here?

He was going to find out today. They'd talk about serious things, and then he'd kiss her.

Maybe too much for a Friday afternoon, he thought, but that didn't stop him from standing and sweeping one arm around her, a smile already on his face.

"I was thinking somewhere off the beaten path today," he said. "What do you think?"

"I think I have a dozen phone calls to make this afternoon," she said. "So wherever this other path is, it better be nearby."

Translation: quick and easy. And that didn't sound conducive to a nice, slow, romantic meal where they could share important things.

Surprise flowed through him that he even wanted a meal like that. His last several dates hadn't exactly encouraged him to keep dating, and Nicole obviously had something about him she didn't like.

"Maybe another time, then," he said. "Let's hit that food truck rally that's in the park."

She smiled at him, her eyes the color the grass should've been, and said, "I want to try that chicken cone truck."

Boone took her hand in his. "Chicken cone truck? Tell me more about this."

"Oh, you'll see." She wore a devilish look in her expression that only made Boone's pulse accelerate. He drove them the few blocks from the run-down building that housed Puppy Pawz and found a spot to park.

It seemed like every family had decided lunch from a food truck in the park was a good idea, because they had to fight a crowd to even get close to a menu.

"It's over there," she said, indicating a bright red truck with a cartoon chicken on it. The animal held an ice cream cone dripping with what looked like vanilla ice cream and caramel sauce.

But as they got closer, Boone could easily see how

wrong he'd been. "Is that...chicken in that waffle cone?" He glanced at Nicole, barely long enough to see her reaction. "With mashed potatoes and gravy?"

"Yes," she said. "And I never get to eat food like this. Come on." She increased her pace and they joined the line for a chicken and mashed potatoes ice cream cone, a twisted version of chicken and waffles Boone was also curious to try.

"Because of your mom?" he asked. "Is that why you don't get to try food like this?"

"Yes," she said simply. She cleared her throat. "And I, um, don't date."

That got Boone's full attention. "You don't date?"

She shook her head. "Not for a while now, no."

Boone squeezed her hand and continued to study her, sure this woman had to turn down dinner invitations left and right. "Why not?"

"No one is interested." A worried look paraded across her face, almost like she expected Boone to bolt at any moment.

His curiosity reached peak levels. "Well, now I find that hard to believe."

"What? That no one is interested."

"Yes," he said.

"Well, *you* weren't interested."

Boone wasn't sure if he should laugh or get offended. It took him a moment to get a proper breath, and when he did, he asked, "You weren't exactly nice to me, you know."

He didn't want to accuse her of anything, but she hadn't been nice.

Nicole looked away, and he disliked the trepidation in her eyes before he couldn't see them anymore.

"Why is that?" he asked. "I've thought a lot about it this week, and I can't figure out what I did to you."

"Nothing," she said, the word carrying a lot of her previous bite. Oh, this tone he was very familiar with, and he didn't like it at all. Not one little bit.

It was almost their turn to order, and Boone swallowed, wondering if this would be their last date. Sort of date. They hadn't exactly defined what they were doing with all these lunches and the hand-holding.

But surely she knew he was interested. Didn't she?

Help me know what to say, he prayed, and he opened his mouth without anything planned in his head.

"I'll figure it out," he said. "But it sure would be easier if you just told me."

Chapter Ten

Nicole's appetite for the fried chicken in a waffle cone had fled about the time Boone had asked "You don't date?" in such an incredulous tone.

As if she were lying to him. As if she had men beating down her door every night.

The very idea was laughable. Most men in this town didn't even know she existed.

And no, she hadn't been nice to him, and she needed to do something about it. An apology. An explanation. Maybe she should even beg for his forgiveness.

Problem was, she didn't want to admit to him that she'd tried to buy the clinic and couldn't get the funding. It was a blow that still hit her hard in the lungs, making it hard to breathe and talk normally.

So she squeezed his hand and said, "I'll tell you soon."

He inched forward in the line, and it was almost their

turn. "Does that mean you'll maybe come to dinner at my place tonight?"

"Tonight?" She looked fully at him, which was probably a big mistake. His eyes were so dark and so dreamy, and she couldn't look directly at him without getting stunned. "I don't think I can tonight."

"What are you doing?"

"Just going to see my parents."

"After that then."

Nicole looked at him, wondering if he really was interested in her. He certainly seemed to be. She reached up with her free hand and cradled his face.

"You really want to?" she asked.

"Why is that a surprise to you?"

She'd already told him she didn't date. "It just seems odd, don't you think?" she asked. "We've worked together for a year, and there's never been this —" She silenced her voice before she could give validity to the very strong and hot spark between them.

"This what?" he asked, half a frown sitting between his eyebrows.

"This...thing between us."

Boone shrugged. "Sometimes God works in mysterious ways." He stepped up to the window and ordered two of their cones, paid, and moved aside.

She went with him, enjoying the width of his shoulders and steadiness of his character. What she used to find annoying, she now found attractive. What she'd once found irritating, she found exciting.

And what had changed? She'd worn her hair down to the dog park and spoken kindly to him?

"You still running?" she asked.

"Every day." He met her eye and added, "I hope my family will come watch me run in the Amarillo marathon."

He'd said his father wasn't happy with him for leaving his hometown but that his siblings and mother supported him. "You don't think they will?"

"I haven't told them about it."

"It's coming up, isn't it?"

"Oh, I've got time." He looked like he wanted to say more, but he didn't. Nicole knew what he wanted. He wanted her to share something real about her life with him, the way he'd done with her.

She'd told him about her parents. But she'd said nothing of her siblings, or how she'd felt overlooked her whole life, or her extreme phobia of singing in public.

"What are you scared of?" she asked, drawing another surprised look from him.

"Scared?" he repeated. "Oh, okay. Let's see. Rattlesnakes." He held up a finger for each item he listed. "Drowning. Making a mistake in the operating room." He stilled and looked at her with a measure of vulnerability she hadn't seen before.

"Boone," the girl called out of the window, and he moved to collect the two chicken cones from her. He returned to Nicole with a massive smile and handed her one.

Her own excitement at the new meal had her smiling too, but she knew it was more because of the man she was with than anything else.

They didn't exactly fit in the park, him wearing his white shirt and tie, a pair of slacks and those shiny black shoes and her in her pink scrubs. But no one gave them a second glance as they wandered over to an available bench and sat down with their food.

Nicole wondered when her life had become this. Become more than dashing out to pick up a salad from the grocery store and eating it alone at her desk. Become something she dreamed of having instead of something she survived.

And she wanted to tell Boone why she'd been mad at him and maybe a little bit nasty to him when he'd come to Three Rivers and the animal hospital.

She dipped a piece of fried chicken into the mashed potatoes and gravy and took a bite, a moan coming out of her throat at the salty, crunchy, meaty flavor.

"Oh, yeah," she said around her mouthful of food. "This is good."

He laughed and took his own bite, his eyes rolling back into his head. She swallowed and joined her laughter to his, vowing to tell him why she'd been a beast to him later.

* * *

NICOLE ARRIVED AT HER PARENTS' house by five-thirty, like clockwork. She heaved herself from her sedan and gave it an affectionate pat as she went around the hood. The smell of something burnt met her nose before she'd even reached the steps leading to the front door. She increased her pace.

"Daddy?" she called as she entered the house. Different scents assaulted her, from the burnt toast to vomit to old plastic. She covered her nose as she gagged. "Mama?"

Her mother hadn't moved from the living room in months. Nicole tried to get her up and walking at least once a week, but her pain had grown and her dementia worsened so that she usually just sat in her recliner and watched game shows. At night, Nicole would tell her about the animals at the clinic, how her mother's friends were doing, and anything else she'd heard around town. It wasn't like her mom listened anyway.

But now the house was empty. Frantic, Nicole scanned the living room. The vomity, bodily fluid smell came from the recliner, and she gagged again as she passed it. The evidence of the burnt toast still sat in the appliance in the kitchen. "Dad?" she called again.

She checked the three bedrooms, and the bathroom, the backyard, and the basement. They simply weren't there.

She pulled out her phone and dialed the only doctor in town. No one answered, but an on-call number was given. She recited it under her breath a couple of times before hanging up and then punching the number in.

No one answered. Desperation clogged her throat. What was the point of an on-call number if the doctor wasn't going to answer?

She turned in a circle, trying to think. Could she call one of her siblings? What would they even do? They'd abandoned her here—the youngest sibling who didn't know any better—to take care of their aging parents.

Anger built with the panic in her chest, flooding her head and making thinking almost impossible.

She was so, so angry she was here alone, dealing with this alone.

It made everything hard, and maybe some of that anger had transferred over to the clinic...and to Boone.

But her siblings could wait. Her anger had to be shelved. Her reasons for treating Boone badly would have to wait to be sorted out.

Right now, she needed to find her mother. Her eyes landed on the house next door, and she practically ran in that direction.

Her parents had lived on this street for over fifty years, and so had a couple of other people. *Bonus of a small town*, she thought as she mounted the steps at the Bates'. She knocked, her fist sounding so loud in the summer evening quiet.

Right when Nicole was about to beat the door down, Mrs. Bates finally opened it. "Oh, Nicole. There you are. I was watching for your car, but I must've missed you."

"My mom?" Nicole asked, her heart racing and not only from the running.

"She got sick this afternoon, and your dad took her to the hospital in Amarillo. They said they'd call."

Nicole started nodding, little short bursts of head movement. "Thank you, Mrs. Bates." She turned to go, barely able to see more than five feet in front of her. Her mind raced. Her parents often went to the hospital in Amarillo instead of the one here, because her mother's specialists were there.

It was just so far from Three Rivers. Could she take tomorrow off work? Should she call Boone now and tell him? What about her dogs? They needed to be fed and taken out. Her stomach roared for food, but she didn't think she'd be able to eat anything right now anyway.

"Hey, are you okay?"

She froze at the deep, sexy, familiar voice. She swallowed and everything came into focus—including Boone standing next to her car.

"What are you doing here?"

"I went to your place to see if you were home and would go to dinner with me." He reached for her. "What's wrong?"

She let him gather her into his strong arms. She let out a few tears though she wished she could hold them back, be strong. She'd never felt so alone as she had thirty seconds ago, and there was Boone, telling her it would be okay, that he'd help her.

"What do you need?" he asked. "Is your mom okay?"

Nicole drew in a deep breath and put some space between them. He kept his warm hands on her arms as she shook her head. "She's in the hospital. I need to go find out what's going on. Neither of my parents have a cell phone."

"I'll drive you," he said.

"I need someone to go take care of Valcor and Taz," she said.

"I'll do it," he said. "And then I'll meet you at the hospital."

"You don't—"

"I'll bring you something to eat." He turned and opened her car door but hesitated before stepping back. "You sure you're okay driving?"

She honestly wasn't sure. And would it really matter if she arrived at the hospital thirty minutes later? A fresh set of tears stained her face, and Boone closed her car door. "I'm driving," he said in that authoritative, bossy voice she hated.

"I'm fine," she said, a bite to her own voice now.

"Uh huh." He steered her toward his much nicer truck. "We'll swing by your place and take care of the dogs. We'll grab something to eat on our way out of town. It'll take ten extra minutes."

"Boone, I said I was fine." She pulled her arm away from his hand, everything in her igniting. "You're not the boss of me. Not right now." She glared up at him with anger coursing through her. It felt unreasonable, but it was there, burning, boiling, bubbling through her.

"You're not fine to drive almost an hour by yourself." He glared right back, the danger in his eyes surely much more impressive than hers. "I want to help. Why are you fighting me on this?"

She had no idea. "Fine." She marched around the front of his truck and climbed in the passenger side. She clenched her arms across her middle and scowled when he got in.

"Fine," he said in a much softer tone and started the truck. "What do you like to eat?"

She remained silent, her emotions clashing and coiling every other second.

Boone didn't push her. He simply drove to her house, went inside and came out with both dogs tucked under his arm. She took them from him, drawing some measure of comfort from them as he once again put the truck in drive.

He pulled into an apartment building in the ritzy part of town before she said, "Where are we?"

"Dylan's going to take the dogs for the night," he said. "He already has Vader and Leia." He reached for her pets, but she cradled Valcor close to her throat.

"Sweetheart, we can't take the poodle to the hospital." He spoke in such a gentle voice, that she passed Valcor over to him, wishing she could tell him that the little dog was a security blanket for her.

She said nothing as she passed over her two dogs and watched as Boone disappeared into the building.

She closed her eyes and prayed. Prayed that Mama would be okay. That her father could be strong. That she could provide the support they needed.

That she could be strong enough to tell Boone the truth about why she hadn't liked him.

Something snaked through her, clearing out all the panic, the fear, the desperation. Peace descended and for that brief moment, Nicole knew that God was with her. That He cared about her, and that whatever happened was in His hands.

Boone returned, and Nicole scooted over on the bench seat to sit right next to him. "I'm sorry," she whispered. "I was freaking out."

He threaded his fingers through hers and held on tight. "It's okay."

She shook her head, trying to make her thoughts align. They moved so quickly from Boone, to her siblings, to her parents, she couldn't make heads nor tails of them.

"I think I blame you for things I shouldn't." The quaking returned to her chest as the words she needed to say built up inside.

And she didn't think she could hold them back this time.

Chapter Eleven

"What kind of things?" Boone asked, his curiosity and his desire for Nicole piqued. Even in her distress, she was beautiful. A fragile soul he wanted to comfort and protect. A fiercely strong woman he wanted to witness take down the world.

"Family things," she said. She didn't say more, and Boone didn't press for details. He sent a silent prayer of gratitude that he'd been prompted to go see her that night despite asking her to dinner at lunchtime and getting a noncommittal answer. And that when he didn't find her at home, he'd called Joanne to find out where her parents lived.

In any other situation, he might have considered his actions on the stalker side, but given the circumstances, he felt sure God had directed him that evening.

"Tell me about your family," he said. "You mentioned your siblings are a lot older than you?"

"I'm angry at them," she said, her voice weary.

He glanced at her and found her eyes closed. Her breathing had evened as well. Her fight or flight adrenaline had calmed. He focused on the road again, a rush of adoration painting his insides with warmth.

"Why?" he asked.

"They left me here to deal with everything," she said.

"Are you going to call them?"

"Later."

Boone swallowed, his need to know overwhelming his desire to keep Nicole close. "Is that why you've been angry with me for so long? Because of them?"

She nodded, the movement soft against his bicep. "I—I don't know why," she said. "But...I think I somehow transfer some of my anger with them onto you."

Boone nodded like he understood, but he didn't. He'd never done anything to her—well, besides his messy handwriting and missing those check boxes he didn't know about. He didn't want to push her farther away, but if this relationship was going to continue, he needed to know.

"Why are you angry with me?" he asked.

She didn't answer, and Boone dared to take his eyes off the road to look at her again. She'd fallen asleep. He chuckled softly, gripped the steering wheel, and decided to let her have a few minutes of peace.

Once they arrived at the hospital and he parked,

Nicole straightened like she'd been shot out of a cannon. "I fell asleep."

"You sure did." He gazed at her. "Are you going to freak out again?" He dealt with a lot of stressed pet owners, and he wanted to be prepared for another episode if it was coming.

She looked back at him, her eyes soft around the edges. He couldn't seem to look away, and something formed between them. Something strong and viable that Boone felt in his own pulse.

He reached up and brushed the wispy pieces of her hair from her forehead. "Nicole, I think you're really pretty," he whispered.

She blinked at him. His heartbeat pulsed, pulsed, pulsed. The moment lengthened, and he leaned closer. "Am I allowed to kiss you?"

She pulled in a breath and the slight upward curve of her lips told Boone *yes. Yes, please kiss me.*

He leaned forward, wondering if this was really where he was going to kiss her for the first time. But he wanted this kiss, had been dreaming about it for a few days now.

The spark she'd been unwilling to name in the park earlier flamed between them, and he was a fraction of an inch from touching his mouth to hers when her phone went off.

She startled and glanced down at her lap. Boone cleared his throat and straightened as she said, "It's the hospital. Hello?"

He couldn't hear the other end of the conversation, but he'd met with enough nervous pet parents to know that the news she was getting wasn't the best.

She hung up and he ran his fingers through his hair. "Should we go in? What did they say?"

"They were just calling to let me know she's here," she said, reaching for the door handle. "They said to check in at the reception desk on the first floor, and they'll tell me which room."

"All right. Let's go find out about your mom." He dropped his hands and turned to exit the truck. She followed him, tucking her hand into his as they entered the hospital.

He stood by her side as she inquired about her mother, got a room number, and walked toward the elevator. Once on the right floor, Boone fell back and let her talk to the nurse alone. She glanced over her shoulder at him, a shy look on her face, before ducking into the appointed room with the nurse.

Boone finally released the breath he hadn't known he'd been holding. He turned away from the nurses' station and went back out to the main hallway. He needed coffee and something to eat. They were going to pick something up on the way, but then she'd fallen asleep.

He didn't want to leave her there without letting her know. He paced back onto the floor and walked the circuit twice before she came out. She'd clearly been crying, and he stepped right into her personal space.

"How is she?"

"She's stable. Daddy fed her some cottage cheese that was sour. She vomited and he panicked and brought her here." She took a deep breath and embraced him. He slid his hands down her back. "She's fine. They're keeping her overnight because she needs the fluids."

"So crisis averted, right?" Boone didn't want to downplay her feelings, but he didn't want to see her worry anymore.

"For now," she said.

"Should we go eat? I hear hospital cafeterias actually have good food."

She laughed in his arms, and Boone wanted that to happen again. And again.

"I need chicken noodle soup," she said. "Do you think they have that?"

"One way to find out." Boone threaded his fingers through hers and led her toward the elevator bank.

A week, then two, passed with Boone paying closer attention to his weekly paperwork and handwriting, which gave him a headache that bordered on a migraine. He'd gotten them in college as he struggled to study for tests and absorb large amounts of printed material. He massaged his temples and took the pain medication the doctor gave him.

"You okay?" Nicole leaned in his doorway late on

Thursday night, the trip to the hospital almost three weeks old.

"Yeah." He smiled and gestured for her to come in. She shut the door behind her, the clinic having closed ten minutes ago. "Why are you still here?"

She gave him a coy smile and sat down in the single chair across from his desk. "Didn't want to go home alone."

"That sounds scandalous." He grinned at her and winced as pain shot up into his brain.

She laughed, which he usually enjoyed, but tonight, with his head pounding, the sound pierced his eardrums. "I'm not a bad cook, and I put everything in the crock pot to make turkey chili this morning. I can whip up some cornbread and we'll be good to go. If you want to come over and eat."

He'd never gotten her to come to his place, and their relationship had been running on a hamster wheel. She'd been adamant about keeping their personal relationship off the clock, and he'd been forced to try to take his lunch at the same time as her, message her once he got home, or take her to dinner a couple of times.

He stood and shrugged out of his lab coat, hanging it on a hook to his right. "I'm good to go now." He glanced at the paperwork he'd been laboring over. "Can I get this to you in the morning?"

She smiled and picked it up. "I'm sure it's fine." She tucked it under her arm and turned toward the door.

Before she could open it, he pressed one palm against it. "Are we off work?" He'd gone to her house a couple of times after dinner, always walking her right up to the front porch and lingering. She had an immaculate front yard, but she'd never invited him inside. He hadn't invited her to his house—yet—because she had barriers up he was still trying to break down.

"We're in the building," she said.

"But we're not working," he argued.

"I'm holding your paperwork."

He took it from her and tossed it back onto his desk. "I'm not wearing my lab coat." He put both hands on either side of her head and leaned toward her. "Come on, Nicole. We're closed." He kicked a grin in her direction, and she melted.

"I guess we're not at work right now."

His smile widened and his pulse kicked into high gear. "You have to know I'm dying to kiss you." His voice came out as barely a whisper.

"Do I?" she teased him, a sliver of fear in her expression that disappeared the longer he looked at her.

"Nicole." He dropped his eyes to her mouth and when he looked at her again, her eyes were closed. She was waiting.

Boone was tired of daydreaming and waiting. Holding her hand and waiting. Eating with her and waiting.

He closed the distance between them and touched his mouth to hers. The spark he'd been imagining roared to life, no longer just a fantasy. This real-life version of kissing her was at least a hundred times better than his own imagination.

Her fingers trailed up his sideburns and along the shaved short part of his head, lighting every sensitive nerve in his scalp on fire. He growled, pulled back the teensiest bit, his breath coming quick, quicker, and kissed her again.

She giggled as soon as she pulled away from him, ducking her head so his mouth met her forehead. He kissed her there, pure delight pulling through him. He chuckled too. "Nicole."

She lifted her head and looked at him. He cupped her face in one of his palms and breathed in with her, his headache starting to subside as the drugs worked their magic.

"Is turkey chili actually good?" He left his office with her right behind him.

"Yes." She scoffed. "Don't be too closed-minded about it. Accept it's turkey and not beef, and you'll be fine."

He pulled her close, already wanting to kiss her again, as they walked down the hall and outside.

"You want to drive with me?" he asked. "I can bring you back here after we eat." He paused, his keys out and his truck just two spots down.

"We're going to my place," she said. "It's just down the street. So just follow me."

Boone agreed, though he wanted to stay with her, even for a five minute drive down the street. He wasn't sure why. Kissing her had definitely changed his life. Changed their relationship.

But is she ready? he wondered, the headache back and pounding furiously against his temples. He pushed the negative thought away and parked behind Nicole in her driveway. She didn't take him directly into the house, but through the gate on the north side.

"Have I told you that I host weddings back here?" She paused at the corner of the house as the most magical backyard came into view.

Boone said, "Wow," and couldn't take in the greenery fast enough. "This is like the Garden of Eden."

She laughed and slipped her hand into his. "I told you I like to garden."

"Weddings, huh?" he said, his mind now racing around the idea of marriage. Would she get married back here? Had she even thought about it?

Don't say anything, he told himself. They'd been dating for four weeks and just had their first kiss. It was much too soon to even mention the M-word. Or the L-word. Or any other relationship word. And besides, the panic now parading through him testified that he wasn't ready for such topics either.

"I have one at the end of the month," she said. "I don't do much but attend, but I was wondering if you'd like to come with me."

He tore his gaze from the magnificence of the orchard to peer down at her. "To a wedding?"

"It's someone I've known my whole life," she said. "I don't want to go alone."

"You realize this means everyone in town will know we're dating. I mean, a *wedding*."

"They already know," she said.

"What?" He hadn't heard anything, but Boone wasn't really a regular in the gossip circles around Three Rivers.

"Joanne knew the morning we went to the pancake house."

Ah, the pancake house. Sandy. He'd forgotten about that, as they hadn't spent any more mornings eating breakfast together. They had been at the dog park, holding hands, and church together too.

"Does that bother you?" she asked.

"Why would it bother me?" He went with her as she moved toward the patio furniture on a bricked in area. "You're the one who wanted to keep everything separate."

"I thought it would make things at the clinic awkward." She shrugged and sat on a bench covered in blue and orange pillows.

He settled next to her and lifted her wrist to his lips. "But it hasn't."

They gazed into her backyard, with its tall, private fences, until she said, "Do you ever worry about what other people think of you?"

"Sure," he said, wondering where this line of thought had come from. "I think everyone does."

"You seem really confident. I wish I felt like that."

"Is this about Pastor Scott pressuring you to sing in the choir?" He couldn't think of much else she needed to worry about in that department.

"I just don't think I can do it."

"Maybe you could try singing for me," he said.

"That's absolutely not going to happen." She pulled her hand away and stood. "I need to get the dogs."

"Nicole."

She paused at the French doors, half-twisted back to him, but didn't fully look at him. "I've already heard you sing at the clinic, remember?"

"That's not really singing." She entered the house, her decision obviously final.

Boone sighed and appreciated the beauty of this oasis. But he wanted more than external beauty. He liked Nicole—at least as much as he knew about her. But he wanted her to open up to him, really *be* with him.

"Well," he said to the garden. "Maybe turkey chili will do the trick."

Chapter Twelve

Nicole puttered around the house on Saturday morning, vacuuming and picking up clothes and shoes she'd left out all week. She'd finally invited Boone over, finally had him enter her quaint cottage. He'd filled it with his broad shoulders and tall frame, his hearty laugher and quick wit.

He'd kissed her in the kitchen after she fed him, in the living room before saying good-night. He seemed genuinely interested in her, and that was the real problem.

No one had ever seemed interested in her.

"There's definitely something wrong with him," she muttered as she ran a duster across her entertainment center. But what it was, she hadn't been able to figure out yet. And she'd been trying, digging up anything she could about him. She'd come up with nothing.

He really did go fishing or horseback riding on the

weekends sometimes. He hung out with Dylan and they watched sports. He was a great veterinarian. Everyone in Three Rivers seemed to love him, even the motel manager who had a reputation for not liking anyone.

He had no criminal record, and the only flaw she could find was some speeding tickets—which he'd paid—from years ago down in Hill Country.

"That's it," she said to the silent house. Taz lifted his head like she was talking to him. "He's *too* perfect. How am I supposed to live with that?"

Her prior opinion of his arrogance had vanished the more she'd gotten to know him—and the more she'd realized how much her attitude toward him wasn't warranted, that it should be directed at her siblings who'd abandoned her in Three Rivers. Or to her situation in caring for her mother. Or to her own lack of training and financial ability to buy the animal hospital.

She shook her head and started singing the song that had been in her head that morning. "Somewhere, over the rainbow...." She really let herself belt out the lyrics, singing in the clear, contained voice she never let loose, never let anyone else hear.

A measure of joy infused her soul as she freed herself from the box where everything got held so tightly. The song finished, and some of her happiness ebbed away with the last note still hanging in the air.

Why can't I sing like that in front of people? she wondered. Pastor Scott had cautioned her about not using her talents. Not sharing them with the world. Nicole felt like she'd never shared anything of worth with the world.

"Do you think God gave you this gift only to hide it?" the pastor had asked.

Nicole had been thinking about his words ever since. She'd been going to choir practice every Wednesday night and every Sunday morning. But she simply could not get herself up to the choir seats when it was time to sing in church, with real people sitting in the rows, listening.

One reason was because Boone had been attending church with her for the past few weeks. She still sat in the third row, sometimes with her father, sometimes not. Boone didn't come early, and he slipped onto the end of the bench beside her like a phantom.

Afterward, he always wanted to go to the park, hold her hand, and talk about what Pastor Scott had said.

She stepped onto the back patio and breathed in the fragrance from her fruit trees, everything simple in the yard. She could brace tree limbs, no problem. She could fertilize a spot of earth where nothing grew. She could look at a rose bush and see what was wrong with it.

Why couldn't she diagnose her own ailments and fix them? She sat on the bench where she and Boone had eaten turkey chili on Thursday night, trying to find the scent of his cologne in the cushions next to her. It wasn't there, but his challenge to sing for him still lingered in her ears.

Help me to trust him, she prayed, her eyes drifting

closed. She couldn't conjure up any more words to add to the prayer, but she didn't need more.

She knew what she needed to do. Now she just needed to do it.

"After I check on Mama." She sighed, stood, and left her backyard to the summer sunshine, the thought of trusting her singing to Boone almost more than she could bear.

* * *

ANOTHER SUNDAY PASSED. Another choir practice. Two more Wednesdays. Everything in her life seemed plugged up. She liked holding Boone's hand, and kissing him, and spending time with him and his dogs.

But things felt like they'd gone as far as they were going to go. She felt stalled, like maybe his interest in her had waned now that he'd spent quite a bit of time with her.

Thursday came again, their longest day. Boone leaned in her doorway, knocking against the frame. "Dinner tonight? My place?"

She glanced up, shock traveling through her that he'd blatantly asked in front of Joanne, who sat no less than six feet from where he stood, a clipboard at his side. She needed to get over her phobia of other people knowing about their relationship. She wasn't embarrassed about it, and the entire town knew anyway.

"Your place?" She stood and came around her desk, this invitation to his personal space new. "You don't cook."

"No, I don't. But I checked on that new open oven pizza place, and they're open late. I know you like pepperoni with extra cheese." He singsonged the last two words, a smile making his good looks downright delicious.

She returned it and pressed one palm against his chest. "Sounds great."

He leaned forward and jerked back. "Great. When's your lunch?"

"Half an hour?"

He looked at his clipboard. "No can do. An hour?"

"I can wait another hour to eat."

He grinned, brushed her hair back in a tender gesture, and left her office. Joanne met her eye, a knowing smile on her face. Nicole returned it, the song in her head now louder than ever.

When a man loves a woman....

But Boone did not love her. She knew, like she knew the sky was blue.

She was still struggling to believe he liked her, but all the signs pointed to the fact that he did.

One step at a time, she told herself and went back to work.

SHE PULLED into Boone's driveway on the north end of town, her stomach a knotted mess. She'd always thought him way out of her league, and this house proved it. Sure, she'd been here before, but she'd been distracted by the huge trucks and the other blonde woman.

The house had a stone and stucco exterior only found in the newer, nicest houses in Three Rivers. A double-car garage, and a yard he clearly paid someone else to maintain. She knew, because it held no personal touch in the mound of flowers in the front yard and the single birch tree near the back fence.

Go on, she told herself when Boone opened the front door and stepped onto the stoop. She'd been coaching herself a lot lately, trying to do things she'd never done before, because she'd never dated a man like Boone before.

She got out of the car and put a smile on her face. "I'm so nervous," she admitted as she went up the four steps and entered his arms.

"Why?"

"This feels like a big step," she said. "Coming to your place."

"I'm not going to bite," he teased. "And the pizza's already here."

She stepped back and smoothed down her scrubs. "I want to do something." She swallowed, her throat as dry as the Sahara. When had she swallowed cotton?

But she needed to do this, do *something.* She wanted

things to move forward with Boone, and she felt like she was the one holding them back.

"Should we eat first?" He gestured toward the house and turned to enter it.

She went with him, trying not to notice the tile, the hardwood floors, the granite, the clean, crisp, contemporary lines.

"No," she said, her tongue so thick in her mouth. "If we eat first, I won't do it."

Boone leaned against the counter next to two pizza boxes. "All right."

She blinked at him, the song she'd chosen to sing for him rebounding from one side of her mind to the other.

He folded his arms and smiled. "Should I keep waiting?"

"Yes," she snapped, her nerves and her hunger making her patience thin. "Do you have any water?"

He pushed away from the counter and retrieved a water bottle from the fridge. He passed it to her with a sexy look on his face that nearly undid her resolve.

"I don't know what you're going to do," he said. "But I'm intrigued."

She took a couple of gulps and set the water bottle next to him. "There." It tipped but didn't fall over and she withdrew from him a few paces. Drew a deep breath. Kept her back to him.

And started singing.

Chapter Thirteen

B oone couldn't believe the beautiful sound that flowed from Nicole's body. She didn't even seem to be trying, and he knew he'd never truly heard her sing around the clinic. That had been muttering. Maybe even just her normal speaking voice compared to the joy pouring from her.

He moved to stand in front of her, and he found the happiest expression in her eyes he'd ever seen on a human being. She finished the song, the last note still bouncing around his fourteen-foot ceilings.

He sucked in a breath, swept into her personal space, and took her face in his hands. He had no words to express how he was feeling in that moment. So he didn't speak. He just kissed her, kissed her, kissed her.

As he did, he fell a little bit more in love with her. He embraced the emotions, because he'd never truly felt them before, and he liked the way they made him feel warm, and happy, and like he didn't have to win a marathon or save an entire herd of cattle to be worthwhile.

"You are magnificent," he whispered when he pulled away. He smiled down at her, letting everything he felt for her stream from him.

"I have terrible stage fright." Her words barely reached his ears.

Boone stepped back and around her to the pizza. He flipped open the box and lifted out a piece of all-meat pizza. "You know, I don't think you do."

She sidled up next to him and glared. "Oh yeah? You know how I feel now?"

He took a bite of his pizza, the conversation he'd had just before she arrived bouncing around in his brain. He needed to tell her about it, but this seemed more important. "Of course not," he said. "But I think you're so used to being overlooked that you think you deserve it."

He bit off the corner of his pizza and chewed while she gaped at him. He didn't want to drive her away, and heaven knew he didn't like it when his father tried to tell him how he felt, as if Boone couldn't make sense of his own emotions.

He leaned closer, hoping she heard what he was going to say. "But I *see* you, Nicole. I always have, even when you weren't very nice to me." He took another piece of pizza, put it on his plate, and parked himself on the couch in front of the TV.

He'd left the conversation open for her to really tell him why she had treated him badly in the beginning, but she didn't. She'd pushed through one door, but expecting her to throw open two was probably too much for a single evening.

He sighed and said, "You deserve to be up in that choir stand, singing the solos." He bypassed the sports channels in favor of the cooking show he knew Nicole liked.

Nicole joined him, way down at the other end of the couch from where he wanted her. "I don't think you know me as well as you think you do."

"I know how you like your coffee in the morning, and that it's not the same in the afternoon. I know you eat a chicken chop salad for lunch every Tuesday. I know you're worried about your mama and feel absolutely worthless to help her or your dad. Should I go on?"

She gestured for him to do so, as if the things he knew about her were easily obtained. But Boone had probed, observed, and listened to learn everything he had about Nicole.

"I know you have a short temper, but hardly anyone gets to see it. I know—"

"Stop it." She put her pizza on the end table next to the couch and picked up the throw pillow his designer had matched with the furniture. "Stop—it—right—now." She punctuated each word with a whack from the pillow, a huge smile on her face.

"I'm apparently the only one on the receiving end of

the temper." He grabbed the pillow on her next swing and laughed, pulling her onto his lap. "I'll admit, I kinda like it."

She squirmed in his arms, but he held her fast. "You do?"

The moment lengthened, and Boone didn't know how to make her believe that he liked her. Kissing her didn't seem to do it. Maybe saying it outright would.

"Yes, Nicole. I like *you*."

A smile bloomed on her face slowly, like one of her midnight orchids she'd told him about. He saw each ray of happiness as it touched her face, and he ran his fingers through her hair.

Her eyes closed, and Boone touched his lips to hers for only a moment. "I got a phone call a few minutes ago I wanted to talk to you about." His stomach rejected the food though he hadn't eaten for hours, and he forced himself to lay very still.

Nicole opened her eyes and looked at him, a hint of anxiety in her expression and her voice when she asked, "Who called?"

"A veterinary friend of mine—Doctor Drew. He's starting a veterinary practice in Amarillo, and he wants me to be his partner."

Her beautiful eyes rounded and her earlier emotion bled into shock. Her hands stilled on his shoulders. "What are you going to do?"

He exhaled. "Two months ago, I would've been packed by now and on the road in the morning."

"You don't like your job here?"

"I love my job here." He kissed her quick on the lips. "Before though, the office administrator would've helped me pack in the blink of an eye, glad to be rid of me."

Regret lanced through her expression. "I thought you were making my job more difficult on purpose."

"Why would I do that?" he asked as she relaxed into his embrace, thinking he was finally going to get some answers.

"I could barely read what you wrote half the time."

"That's because I have dyslexia." Boone had been wondering when he'd tell her, and the words had just appeared, the conversation easier than he'd thought.

She straightened again, her eyes searching his. "I—I don't know what to say."

"You're the only person outside of my family who knows." He stroked her hair away from her face again, and then again. "Do you want to help me pack and boot me to Amarillo?"

He prayed with everything inside him that she'd say no. For the first time in his life, he felt like he'd found somewhere he wanted to stay, with someone he wanted to stay with.

She shook her head, which sent relief cascading through him. "No." She slipped off his lap but stayed next to him on the couch. "What are you going to do?"

"I don't know." He sighed and picked up the discarded pillow, replacing it on the end of the couch where Nicole had originally sat. "It's a good opportunity, but I'm—I think I'm finally happy here."

"You weren't before?"

"There was this Nazi office administrator who—"

"All right." She looked at him and laughed. "I was really awful, wasn't I?"

"Yes, you were." He finished his first slice of pizza. "And I think there's more to it than just transferred anger from your siblings, for the official record."

"You think you're so smart. *That's* one reason for my attitude right there."

"Yeah, I don't think so. I've never seen you give anyone as hard of a time as me."

"That's because you took my job."

All the air rushed out of the Boone's lungs. "What? How? There wasn't a veterinarian in town before I came here. The clinic was going to close."

She folded her hands in her lap and looked at them. "Exactly. I'd been taking online business classes, and I was going to buy the animal hospital."

Boone had no idea what to say. "No one told me that. There wasn't another offer on the table when I offered on the clinic."

"I know."

"Hey." Boone reached for one of her hands and

slipped his fingers between hers. "Can you look at me? Talk to me about this."

She shook her head, her mouth a tight line, and lifted her eyes to meet his.

Helplessness filled him at the pain that swam in her green depths. "I didn't know," he said. "I—" He didn't know what to say.

He'd come to Three Rivers for a couple of reasons, only one of which was the animal hospital. He hadn't told her about the other one quite yet, and he wondered what she'd think of him then.

Before they started dating, he would've taken the knowledge of the misdiagnosis to the grave. But now...now he trusted her and wanted her to know everything about him. The good, the bad, and the painful.

"You just seemed to soar into town on your white horse," she said. "And save the hospital. Everyone talked about you like you were God himself." Nicole's eyes stormed and her bottom lip shook the teensiest bit. "It was easier to dislike you," she admitted. "Until...."

"Until what?"

"I had myself convinced you were a monster until that day in the dog park."

Boone remembered the first time he'd looked at Nicole with the thought that he'd like to get to know her better. "That was a great day, wasn't it?"

She finally allowed a smile to cross her face. "It was a pretty great day. Today doesn't feel like a great day, though." She turned toward him, a muscle in her jaw jumping. "I don't want you to go to Amarillo."

"Well, I'm going," he said. "There's a marathon in February I've been training for." He tossed her a grin and took a huge bite of pizza while she shook her head and laughed under her breath.

"You're impossible," she said.

"Now, the veterinary job is up in the air," he said. "I mean, I have this great house. A job I love. A gorgeous girl-friend...." He glanced at her to judge her reaction.

A smile brightened her face, and Boone tucked her into his side. "I think I should just stay right here for a while. What do you think?"

"I like you right here, yes," she said, and Boone spiraled a little further down the pipeline toward being all the way in love with Nicole Hymas.

The opportunity to be a partner at an animal hospital in a bigger city rolled around in his head as a celebrity chef made a double chocolate cake on the screen in front of him.

He'd have to tell Cash Drew something, but a flat-out no didn't feel quite right. He pulled Nicole closer, the thought of leaving her absolutely wrong too.

* * *

A week later, Boone arrived at Nicole's a full two hours before the wedding was supposed to begin, but there was already a pile of cars taking up the street. So he parked down the block a ways and flung his garment bag holding his tuxedo over his shoulder. He wasn't planning on getting dressed for a while, but when he stepped into Nicole's house and found her bustling around the kitchen in a bright pink party dress, he wondered if he'd gotten the time wrong.

"Hey," he said, stepping into the narrow space and pulling her into him. "Mm." He kissed her, tipping her back until she giggled and swatted at his shoulder.

"That is not proper behavior for a wedding," she said as he brought her back to standing.

"I think it's exactly what people do at weddings," he said. "They dance, they kiss, they go home happy." He lifted the garment bag. "Should I change now? I thought we were finishing the decorations and then fading into the background."

"We are, but then the bride called and asked if she could use my oven to keep some appetizers warm." She arranged tiny little meatballs on a sheet tray, her fingers working double time.

"Why are you doing this in such a sexy dress?" He slid behind her in the tiny kitchen and put his arms around her waist, bending to touch his mouth to the nape of her neck.

She laughed and squirmed away. "Stop it. I'm busy here."

"I can see that." He chuckled, moved back into the

living room, and draped his bag over the back of her couch. "I'll go check the backyard."

"The lights need to be strung in the orchard," she said as he passed her again. "I ran the extension cord already. The lights are on the patio table."

"Lights on the patio table," he repeated and stepped into the backyard. The scene beyond her fence showed one of the most beautiful evening skies he'd ever seen, deep with blue and purple and pink. He took a deep breath and sent a prayer of gratitude for this life he had now.

He thought he'd been happy before, but he'd never known as much joy as he'd experienced in the few months he'd been dating Nicole.

He strung the lights, humming the song she'd sung for him a few weeks ago. He started singing the lyrics, his bass voice nowhere near the right octave. "I feel pretty...."

"You are pretty." Nicole burst into laughter as she joined him in the orchard.

"Almost done," he said. "What's the song for today?"

She slanted a wary look at him. "Want to guess?"

"Sure. Give me a few lines."

She sang the rock lyrics in a rough voice, a slight accent in there he couldn't place.

"*Livin' on a prayer*. Classic." He burst into laughter. "Eighties hair band," he said. "How do you know that song?"

"Remember how all my siblings are ages older than me? That's how."

He brought her close for a kiss and started to sway with her, joining his voice to hers in a slower, softer version of the song. She practically yelled the last line. She trilled out a laugh, and Boone spun her through the grass.

He brought her close again and held her against his body. "I think you're amazing, Nicole."

She froze, her eyes lit by the tiny fairy lights and making her seem softer and more beautiful than ever. He leaned down and kissed her until the fear in her touch evaporated.

But he'd definitely need to figure out what it took to get her to believe that he liked her, because he was already several steps down a path that led to love when it came to Nicole Hymas.

Chapter Fourteen

Nicole had never done drugs or taken a sip of alcohol. But she felt absolutely drunk on the taste, the feel, the scent of Boone Carver.

The man had soared into town on his white horse...but was it to save her? She hadn't even known how lost she was, or how close to the edge of the cliff.

But he'd pulled her back to the land of the living. Shown her what it felt like to actually live—and possibly love.

He broke their kiss first, and Nicole tucked herself right against his chest, imagining this to be their wedding day, and their first dance in her garden though there weren't any guests there yet.

His simple, strong words reverberated through her whole body. *I think you're amazing, Nicole.*

Amazing.

She'd been waiting for so long to feel this strongly about a man. So long for someone to see her, to belong to and with.

He chuckled and swung her in a circle, lifting her off her feet. She squealed and held onto his broad shoulders, wondering if her brothers and sisters would return to Three Rivers for her wedding.

She disliked that they were so present, poisoning her happy moment. She'd called them about Mama's brief hospital stay, but there wasn't anything they could do. Mama had come home the next day anyway.

Boone set her back on her feet and gazed down at her with absolute adoration and joy. She didn't feel worthy of his attention, but she was trying. Since he'd told her she didn't really have stage fright, she'd been spending more time in the scriptures, more time on her knees, but it was hard to undo forty years of mental training.

Every time she went to Boone's place she was reminded of how much more he possessed. Then she'd remind herself that he never seemed to care about her cracker box house, and he'd been working to make sure his paperwork was absolutely right every night before he left, and he'd forgiven her for a year's worth of nastiness.

She really didn't deserve him. *But help me to become the woman who does*, she prayed as she gazed up into the lights in the tree limbs.

"How did Cash take the news that you weren't coming to Amarillo?" she asked.

"Just fine. Said the invitation is always open." Boone inhaled her hair, a gesture of his that made her feel cherished and strong.

"Pastor Scott called and asked me to meet him before church tomorrow," she said.

He stilled, leaned back, his dark eyes staring right through her. "When did that happen?"

"Just this morning."

His eyes widened. "Your self-restraint is amazing. I can't believe you waited until now to tell me."

"I...don't know. What do you think he wants?"

"He's going—"

Behind them, someone called, "Hello?" and Nicole stepped out of his arms. "That must be Heidi with the food."

"The bakery is delivering the food?"

"Your aunt can do everything, Boone," Nicole called over her shoulder as she gained the patio. She swung back to him. "Oh, the arch needs to go up, remember?"

He waved to her and she entered the house to find not only Heidi, but Kelly Ackerman and Chelsea Marshall. In front of them, they had boxes and trays of pastries, and while Nicole knew these women from church, they were several years older than her, with husbands and children and a life on the ranch where Boone worked that she knew nothing about.

Heidi smiled at her and asked, "Where would you like this stuff?"

"Out here." She stepped back to the patio, where she'd set up the refreshment line.

Everyone followed her, their shoes making quite the racket on her deck. Kelly whistled and swiveled her head back and forth. "Wow, Nicole, this is fantastic. Maybe I should've gotten married here."

Nicole turned back to her and smiled. "Please. Like your husband would've driven all this way just to get married."

Kelly laughed and shrugged. "The ranch wedding was nice, but this is like a tropical wonderland."

"Not quite." But Nicole appreciated the sentiment.

"Is that Boone setting up that arch?" Kelly didn't miss much, Nicole would give her that.

"Of course," Heidi said. "I told you they were dating." She beamed at Nicole like she'd tamed a wild lion single-handedly. "Y'all getting along okay?"

"Yes, ma'am," Nicole said, her Texas manners making a sudden appearance.

"Look at him on that ladder," Chelsea said, adding a giggle. "I mean, I've seen Boone do just about everything at the ranch, but settin' up a weddin'?" She looked at Nicole with a mischievous twinkle in her eye. "That man must really like you."

I think you're amazing, Nicole.

Heidi set down her tray of what looked like apricot squares. "Oh, go on, you two. Leave her alone. Kelly, go get the warmers out of the truck, would you? Chelsea, I need the dishes we brought."

Nicole left them to take care of the food, as she certainly wasn't getting paid to do that and she didn't really want to discuss her relationship with Boone with his family. With only a half an hour until the wedding would officially start, she made her final checks on the yard.

"Everything is perfect," she said once she'd gone around and checked lighting, power, and seating.

The bride had arrived and taken over Nicole's spare bedroom, as agreed. The groom was using her bedroom, but he was much quicker, so when Boone returned from taking Taz and Valcor to his place for the evening, she shooed him in there to change also.

He emerged from the bedroom several minutes later, taller and more handsome than when he went in. "You should be illegal," she said as she drank in the tuxedo that had obviously been tailored just for his frame.

She reached up and ran her fingers along the shaved part of his head and into his longer hair, glad she was able to do such things whenever she wanted. The crowds started arriving then, and Nicole faded into the background the way she always did.

Except tonight, with Boone at her side, person after person approached her and said the yard looked wonderful.

"Simply beautiful," Trina said, gripping Nicole's

elbow. "Isn't it great?" she asked Cal and her step-daughter Sabrina, who both nodded.

She basked in the compliments and Boone actually led her through the crowd while they ate to make small talk, something she'd never done at a wedding before. If she wasn't hovering on the cusp of the backyard, she was sitting alone at a table against the wall of the church, wishing she were with her sick mama.

At least that was how the last several weddings she'd attended had gone. Tonight, she felt like a monarch butterfly, finally spreading her great, orange wings and preparing to fly.

Tonight, everything was perfect.

NICOLE ARRIVED at the church the following morning a half an hour earlier than normal. Boone had already texted her—*Call me as soon as you're done*—which had only added fuel to her fiery nerves.

She felt like she might combust at any moment, and then she'd burn the church right to the ground.

Drawing in a deep breath, she brushed imaginary dust from her skirt and started up the sidewalk. This little building near the park in Three Rivers had brought her more comfort over the years than almost anything else.

The only thing she'd been more invested in was Puppy

Pawz, which was why Boone's purchase of it had burned so badly. Perhaps she should've told him that.

She remembered the agony in his eyes when she'd confessed why she'd disliked him so much. Her feelings didn't make sense, she knew that. At least Boone had been forgiving and sensitive, even going so far as to ask her for advice a time or two since their talk last weekend.

He was *trying*, and Nicole could see that. It was something no one else in her life seemed to do. Daddy had let Nicole take over the care of Mama. Her siblings had left town despite their mother's diagnosis.

She pushed Boone out of her mind as her heels clicked through the foyer and down the hall to Pastor Scott's office. She needed a clear head for this conversation, and Boone didn't exactly help her see rationally.

"Good morning," she said, pausing on the threshold of his office and knocking lightly on the doorframe.

He glanced up from the book he had open on the desk in front of him. A moment passed while he looked at her, and then a smile burst onto his face and he leapt to his feet. "Nicole, come in." He came around the desk and shook her hand. "Come in."

She stepped past him, her nerves almost turning to panic. She perched on one of the chairs in front of his desk and put her purse on her lap like it was a shield.

"The wedding last night was wonderful," he said in that voice made of power and honey. "Your yard is beautiful."

"Thank you," she murmured, hoping the small talk would end so she could finally know why he'd called her in here.

He relaxed back into his chair, the joviality still present in his blue eyes. He watched her, clearly not uncomfortable, for several long moments.

She nodded at him to go on, get this over with.

"So I asked you here specifically to invite you to sing in the choir for our Christmas program."

All the air left Nicole's lungs, though she'd suspected it would be something to do with the choir.

"You're coming to practices anyway, and Brother Myron wants you to do the solo part. His wife has written the program, and it's beautiful." Pastor Scott opened a drawer in his desk and pulled out a folder. "It's all here. You can look at it and decide."

Nicole couldn't move, so she just nodded again.

Pastor Scott chuckled, but it wasn't a judgmental laugh or a cruel one either. Everything about him was soft yet strong, exactly how Nicole wanted to be.

"I know you're scared," he said. "But I really think the people of Three Rivers would love to hear you sing."

She nodded again, wondering if that was all she could do anymore. Thankfully, she was able to reach out and take the folder from his desk. "I'll look it over," she managed to push out of her dry throat.

"I supposed that's all I can ask." Pastor Scott leaned back again. "But really, Nicole, you have a beautiful voice, and you shouldn't be hiding your talents from the world."

"I'm not hiding," she said. But was she? Or had she simply been overlooked...again?

"You come to choir practice and don't sing," the pastor said. "What do you call that?"

"Stage fright," Nicole answered, her grip on the folder a little too tight. "I don't think you understand how debilitating it can be."

Pastor Scott at least had the decency to acknowledge what she'd said. He thought for a moment and said, "You're right, I don't. But the Lord does. Ask Him about this and see what He says."

She nodded, stood, and shook the pastor's hand. He wouldn't let go, adding, "There's plenty of time to prepare. Really think and pray about it, okay?"

"Okay," she said and got the heck out of there. Her fingers trembled as she walked back outside and to her car. Though fall had arrived on the calendar, Mother Nature had not gotten the memo.

The heat in the car actually felt good, thawing the icy places inside Nicole that had formed the instant Pastor Scott had said the choir director wanted her to sing the solos.

Solos? She shook her head, a measure of disgust rolling through her. She couldn't even get up and join her voice to thirty others. How did anyone expect her to open her mouth and sing all by herself?

How can I do that? she prayed. I don't think it's possible. But if it is, show me how.

No heavenly vision appeared in front of her. She started the car so she wouldn't bake in the next few minutes before she could go back inside.

She wondered how she could be strong enough to sing in front of everyone, and as the list of reasons why grew, someone knocked on her passenger window.

Boone stood there, gesturing to know if he could come in. She unlocked the doors and he slid into the vehicle with her. All at once, she knew how she could be strong enough.

She'd just pretend she was singing with her back to Boone. She'd done that. He'd given her the strength to do it.

"Hey," he said. "You didn't call, and I saw you sitting here."

She practically lunged across the console, wrapping her arms around him and pressing her mouth sloppily to his. He chuckled, aligned everything, and kissed her until the panicky feeling inside trickled away.

Chapter Fifteen

Boone sensed something new in Nicole's touch. It felt a bit frantic and a bit manic, but he went with it. He knew what Pastor Scott was going to ask her anyway, so he let her kiss him until she pulled away.

She ran her fingers through her hair and sighed. "He wants me to sing the solos in the Christmas program." She indicated a folder she'd tossed up on her dashboard. "I guess they wrote it just for me."

"That's great, Nicole," he said, reaching for the folder. "What do you think?"

"You know what I think. I think I'm going to throw up."

"It's only September," he said, flipping the folder open. "And look, your song of the day last week was *Silent Night*." He tipped the sheet music toward her, but she didn't even glance at it.

Misery rolled off of her in waves, and Boone wished he understood this particular affliction. But he'd never had a problem standing up in front of people and talking. Or singing.

"You can sing for me every night, if you think it will help," he offered. He closed the folder and put it back on the dashboard.

"I don't think that will help."

He reached over and took her hand in his, glad when her initial resistance melted away and she allowed him to lift her fingers to his lips. "What will help, sweetheart?"

She turned and looked at him then, a raw vulnerability on her face he'd never seen before. "I don't know, Boone. Prayer?"

"I can pray for you." He smiled the gentlest smile he could. "Maybe you'd like to come out to the ranch and sing to the horses. They like it."

"Is that what you do when you go out there on the weekends?"

He swallowed, his own fears about to come to fruition. "No." Boone didn't have a plan for this, but maybe blurting it out would be okay. Maybe he could be vulnerable with Nicole while she was completely real with him.

"I go out to the ranch on weekends for equine therapy," he said, the words slow and measured, each one appearing in his mind as he said it.

Her fingers on his tightened. "Really? Therapy?"

"At Courage Reins. The horses...help."

Nicole continued to peer at him, clearly wanting more of the story. Boone's chest tightened, and his memories surged forward.

"They might help you too," he said. "You could come out with me one weekend, if you want. I'm going this Saturday." He went twice a month, and Pete had said he could probably cut back to once.

But Boone liked the therapy sessions. Liked talking to the horses like they could hear him, liked the way he felt calm for days afterward.

"I'd like that," she said. "We'll be late for church."

"Just the opening musical numbers," he said, a sly grin crossing his face. "But it's fine. If you don't want to hear why I'm in horse therapy, that's fine." He reached for the car door handle, but she practically jerked his arm off.

"I want to hear."

Their eyes met, and Boone was struck once again with her beauty. He trusted her when he'd only told this particular secret to Peony before.

"So I came to Three Rivers because of the animal hospital," he said. "But that was only one reason." His brain flowed back a couple of years, and he marveled at how different his life was. Just the fact that he was sitting in a church parking lot was leagues from where he'd been in Temple.

"Anyway." He cleared his throat, realizing this was a story and he had to do all the talking. "Another was my cousin, Squire. He needed help on the ranch, and I figured if the hospital fell through, I'd at least have that."

"You didn't like your family's ranch," she said. "How's this one different?"

"No expectations," he said. "And my father's not here." He didn't let his mind go down that path. "There was a third reason," he said.

Several seconds went by, with only the air conditioner blowing air on them for sound. "Go on, Boone," she said. "I won't judge you."

"You might."

She lifted his hand to her lips this time, and Boone appreciated the gesture and her words when she said, "I won't. I promise."

He pulled in a deep, deep breath. "I had a job in Temple. I was the large animal vet, and I'd make visits to ranches throughout the area. A herd of cattle came down with something, and I...." *Rushed the diagnosis.*

Didn't get all the facts.

Thought I was so smart.

Let my pride get the better of me.

"I misdiagnosed them," he said. "Over five hundred head died before I realized my mistake." He pressed his eyes closed, the memories from that time rushing at him, choking him, drowning him.

Her fingers tightened on his. "Oh, Boone. I'm so sorry."

"I couldn't stay there. I packed in the night and left in

the morning. I came to Three Rivers and stayed at the ranch for a couple of nights and that's when I learned about the animal hospital here."

He looked at her, everything he was feeling simply coming out of him. He didn't know how to hold it back, and he found that with Nicole, he didn't *want* to hold it back.

"My dad told me to come on home and join my brother on the ranch. We fought a little. Not much, because I refuse to engage. That's why we don't get along. He doesn't understand that I'd rather run in the morning and take care of pets and cows in the afternoon."

Nicole gave him a warm, wonderful smile. "It's the running I don't understand."

Boone sucked in a breath and then released everything he'd kept bottled up in a loud laugh. She laughed with him, and the awkwardness and tension between them fled.

"Come on," he said as he caught sight of a family hurrying inside the church. "We don't want to be too late. Then only the front pew will be left."

They got out of the car and walked toward the church hand-in-hand. Nicole paused on the sidewalk and tipped up toward him. He thought she'd kiss him again, which he was more than willing to do, but she simply whispered, "Thank you for telling me."

She settled back onto her feet and looked at him. "Sure," he said, unsure of what else to vocalize.

"I think you're amazing too, Boone." She opened the

door to the church, and Boone followed her inside. Her words rang throughout his whole body, and he had a suspicion he'd follow her anywhere.

He wasn't sure if the thought excited him or terrified him. He simply knew he was moments away from falling all the way in love with her, and that definitely brought a sting of fear to his heart.

* * *

Friday morning, Boone sat in his office, not much on his schedule for the day. No surgeries. Only three appointments. Autumn had definitely hit Three Rivers, and people were back in school and life was humming along.

His mom had texted that morning about the holidays, but Boone wasn't sure what to tell her. He glanced at his phone again, wondering if he dared take the sixteen steps down to Nicole's office and ask her to drive to Grape Seed Falls with him for Thanksgiving.

He wasn't sure what his hesitation was. He'd shared more with her than anyone else, and she indeed hadn't judged him for his mistakes with the cattle in Temple.

Sighing, he got up and started walking. *Step one, two, three....* Sixteen steps later, he arrived in her doorway, and she glanced up at him. Her smile came quickly, and Boone wanted to dart inside, secure the door, and kiss her until he couldn't breathe.

"I have a couple of questions," he said. "First, do you

really want to come out to Courage Reins with me tomorrow? I'd need to call ahead and see if they have a horse for you." He paused, this first question definitely the easiest one for her to answer.

She had not practiced any of the Christmas songs with him, nor had she even brought it up again.

Nicole wiped her hand over her hair, pushing back some of the wisps that had fallen out of her ponytail. "Yes," she said. "I think I'd like to come."

Boone took a step into her office, then another until he could close the door behind him. If Joanne thought it was weird, he didn't care.

Nicole blinked at him, her surprise evident in her gorgeous hazel eyes. "What's going on?" she asked with plenty of trepidation in her voice.

"My mom wants me to come home for Thanksgiving or Christmas. I was—" He cleared his throat, wishing this were easier. He and Nicole had been dating for a while now, but were they to the stage where he took her home to meet his family?

"I was wondering if you felt like...I was thinking... Maybe we should go together."

"Go together to your family's for Thanksgiving?"

"Yeah."

Nicole glanced to the closed door. "I have to tell you something."

Boone leaned forward, interested in anything she had to say. "All right."

"I've never left Three Rivers."

Boone sat back like she'd hit him. "What?"

"I've lived here my whole life," she said, anxiety entering her expression. "And I've never left."

"Well, we went to Amarillo to go to the hospital."

"Yes, I've driven to Amarillo."

"You never went on vacation?" Even though his family had been poor growing up, with most of their money going right back into the ranch, his parents had taken him to Galveston to see the Gulf of Mexico and to California to play in the Pacific Ocean.

"My mother has been sick for a long, long time, and my last sibling left home when I was only seven." The pain behind her words wasn't hard for Boone to hear. In the past, he might have missed it. But not today.

"So we'll go, if you want," he said. "We can tour Hill Country while we're down there. It's beautiful. We can go over to Austin if you want. Go to the Gulf." He raised his eyebrows. "Do you want to travel?"

"Yes," she whispered.

He lifted his phone. "So I'll tell my mom yes?"

"Have you told her about us at all?"

"A little," he admitted. "I told her I was seeing someone. I've never mentioned how serious it was." In fact, he'd like to know how serious they were. "If we go to my family ranch for Thanksgiving, that's serious." He gazed at her, desperate for a label. "Right?"

She swallowed and nodded. "I think that's pretty serious."

"You don't sound happy about it." Boone put a smile on his face. "For the record, I've never taken anyone home to meet my family."

"For the record, I haven't either." She stood and he joined her at the end of her desk. "Tell your mom yes."

"Yeah?"

Nicole tipped up to kiss him, whispering, "Yeah," into his mouth before kissing him again.

Boone lost himself in her touch, glad they were continuing to move forward. Most of his past relationships had stalled at some point, sticking before moving on.

But this thing with Nicole felt like it could expand and grow for years to come, and Boone couldn't wait to introduce her to his family.

Well, maybe not his father, and Boone had the sudden urge to protect her from him as she surely wouldn't be good enough.

Why wouldn't she be good enough? he thought as he stepped away and said he'd go make the phone calls and texts he needed to.

He wasn't sure why Nicole wouldn't meet his father's standards, but the thought gnawed at him while he dialed Courage Reins, and he couldn't be happier he had his therapy riding session tomorrow so he could work through some of his tangled thoughts.

Chapter Sixteen

Nicole woke on Saturday morning with a hive of bees in her stomach. Despite growing up in a small Texas town, she hadn't been on a horse since her childhood riding camp.

And she was going to be riding a lot today, as well as... well, she didn't really know what equine therapy entailed.

When Boone showed up at her house in his huge truck and wearing his cowboy hat, she knew it involved her heartbeat racing around her chest like she'd met a celebrity.

He was just so dang delicious in that hat.

"Am I really bringing Valcor and Taz?"

"Yeah, sure, the dogs just run around out there. They love it." He gestured to the back of his truck, where both of his dogs had their front paws perched on the frame, their eyes eager and their tongues hanging out.

"Valcor weighs six pounds."

"He can hang out in Pete's yard. He's got kids. They'll love him."

Nothing seemed to rattle Boone, and she wondered again why he went out to the ranch for therapy. Of course, he'd told her about the cows he'd lost, and maybe that haunted him more than she knew.

He also didn't have a great relationship with his dad, and Nicole couldn't even imagine what that was like. Her best friends growing up had been her parents and a rose bush, and she suddenly wondered why she hadn't gone out for therapy earlier.

"So I don't have a hat," she said.

"Oh, hang here a sec." He spun away from her and dashed back to his truck. She didn't "hang there," but stepped back inside and told Taz to come while she picked up Valcor.

"We're going out to a ranch," she said. "There are other dogs there, and horses, and cows, and probably some chickens." She met Boone at the bottom of her front steps, and he presented her with a beautiful dark purple cowgirl hat.

"I got this for you."

"When in the world did you get this?"

"Yesterday afternoon, when I left early." He grinned at her. "You seemed like the eggplanty type."

"Don't ever say that again," she said, handing him

Valcor and taking the hat from him. "No woman wants to be told they're the eggplanty type."

He laughed and took the dogs to the back of his truck, helping Taz to jump in with his beasts.

Nicole simply held the hat, wondering how in the world to put it on. When Boone saw her, he chuckled again and said, "It just goes on top, sweetheart." He took it from her and gently pressed it on her head, almost all the way to her ears. "Like that."

"It's a bit...something."

"It'll form to your head," he said. "That's why cowboys don't share hats. They're broken in to our exact head shape and size."

"Really?" She glanced up at his hat. "So you wouldn't let me borrow that?"

He pressed his hat further onto his head. "It would take a mighty act of God."

She laughed, and he helped her into his truck. She slid across the seat so she could sit right next to him on the drive out to the ranch.

"You better tell me a little about your family," she said. "How did your mom take the news that you were bringing your girlfriend?" The word fell from her lips, and she really liked it.

I'm Boone Carver's girlfriend.

She'd never thought those words in that order before, and a rush of warmth filled her from top to bottom.

"She called," Boone said. "Nearly blasted my ear off with a screech."

Nicole laughed. "I'm surprised at that. Seems like a man like you would've had a lot of girlfriends."

"Yeah, maybe," he said and didn't elaborate. "But she was excited. I, uh, haven't been home in a few years."

"I thought you went after the thing in Temple."

"I did. For a night. It's...going there is hard for me. I had a good childhood, don't get me wrong. But." He sighed. "I don't know. It's just too hard to go there and feel like I've let my dad down. It's easier if I just do my own thing."

"What about your siblings? You talk to them?"

"My sister the most," he said. "My older brother just got married, and I was there for that one night. I think that's why my argument with my father was so mild." He made the turn onto the road that led out to the ranch, bypassing the street that went down to his house without even glancing that way.

A few miles went by, indicating that Boone was finished with the family stories.

"So tell me about the therapy," she said, her chest squeezing as she thought about getting on the huge animal.

"It's what you want it to be," he said. "They work with veterans and people with mental disabilities. For people like me, I can walk with the horse. Brush it down. Learn how to take care of it. Ride it. Whatever.

It's just being with the horse that matters, at least to me."

"And you sing to yours."

"Well, *I* don't," he said. "You've heard my terrible singing."

"Oh, come on." She looked at him to make sure he wasn't joking. He didn't seem to be.

"Well, I'm not you, sweetheart." He shook his head and smiled. "I just talk to my horse. I've had a bit of luck with just getting out what I'm thinking to a non-judgmental party."

"What do you tell them?"

"Whatever's bothering me." He cut her a glance. "It's private. That's the whole point."

Nicole took the hint and the rest of the drive happened in relative silence. Her nerves doubled as he turned onto a dirt road and bumped down a ways before rounding a curve.

The ranch spread before her, and Nicole had been out here years and years ago. It was completely different now, what with two houses, and couple of huge stables, and another building that looked like it was made of windows and didn't belong on a ranch at all.

Boone pulled into the parking lot in front of the glass building, and Nicole peered up at it. "This is where we're going?"

"Yeah, this is where we check in." Boone got out of his truck and extended his hand for her to take. She dropped to the ground beside him, and he wrapped one strong arm around her waist, keeping her close as he said, "I'm glad you came today."

He stepped back as quickly as he'd melted her muscles and walked to the tailgate to let the dogs down. He collected Valcor in his arms, but the other pups all jumped down by themselves.

"This way." He kept her poodle and went through the front doors of the building without a backward glance at his dogs as they ran off, Taz in tow.

Nicole watched them go, a tad uncertain about just letting her pug run off on this unfamiliar land. Another dog barked from somewhere over by the original homestead, and Boone said, "You okay, Nicole?"

So she turned and walked past him, hoping she could ride a horse in sneakers.

She took her dog from him while he checked in and got the names of the horses they'd be riding. "So I don't have to ride?" she asked.

"Not if you don't want to," he said, glancing at the man behind the counter. "Reese here can explain more than I can."

The man stood, but he wasn't much taller than sitting. He came around the counter with a very defined limp, a big smile on his face. "Okay, so Boone likes to ride outdoors. Thinks the walls have ears or something."

"Not true," Boone protested, glancing between Reese and Nicole. "I just like the open sky."

Reese chuckled. "Right. You can ride inside or outside. You can stay in the arena and play ball with the horse—yours is named Doughnut—or we can get a cowboy to meet you in the barn, and he'll teach you how to brush down the animal. Really, it's whatever you want." He leaned against the counter and plucked a paper from the other side of it.

"If you'd like a more coordinated care plan, we can set that up too. You'd work with the same horse every time, and you'd have a coordinator and counselor assigned to you to manage the care."

Nicole looked back and forth from Reese to Boone. "I...I want to ride." She wasn't sure where the words came from. "But it's been a long time since I've been on a horse."

"That's fine." Reese smiled, slipping the paper back over the counter. "Let's go out to the barn, and then I'll take your pup over to Pete's." He collected Valcor from her and started down the hallway.

Nicole followed. She listened. She put her foot where the cowboy named Bennett said, and she somehow landed in the saddle on top of a beautiful brown horse named Doughnut.

"All right," Bennett said, swinging onto his horse. "Are we staying in or going out?"

Boone had saddled and mounted his horse, tipped his hat to her, and left several minutes ago. She wasn't sure if she should be alarmed or not. But they weren't in group therapy, and he'd already made it very clear that he liked his private sessions with the horses and the wide open sky.

Nicole gathered her courage and said, "I think outside, if that's okay."

"Sure thing," Bennett drawled, and he led her toward the huge doors at the end of the row. Doughnut simply moved behind his horse, slow and methodical, like he was bored to death.

Outside, everything improved. The sun shone warmly but Nicole enjoyed the feel of it on her bare arms.

Bennett said, "This field is fenced, and you can take as long as you want," before he went back inside and left her alone.

Just her and the horse. Her and this beautiful country. She leaned down and patted Doughnut's neck. "All right, boy. Let's walk."

She nudged her horse the way Bennett had taught her, and Doughnut plodded forward obediently. So maybe this horseback riding thing wasn't so hard.

A measure of pride and accomplishment filled Nicole, and she let Doughnut migrate to the fence and simply walk along it.

She just let the wind whisper, and the horse walk, and her pulse eventually calmed. She felt a keen sense of peace descend upon her, and she hadn't felt this way in a long, long time.

Her life in Three Rivers had always felt caged in. She'd been trapped here since she was old enough to boil water, and the thought of driving several long hours to Hill Country brought a sense of excitement bubbling through her.

"So, I've never left Three Rivers for much of anything," she told Doughnut. "And I get to go to Grape Seed Falls for Thanksgiving. Have you traveled a lot?"

Of course, the horse didn't answer, and Nicole continued on about how excited she was for the trip, to meet Boone's family, and to have a little vacation.

"But really," she said, probably going around for the sixth time. "I'm nervous about leaving Mama and Daddy here for the holidays. I'm sure they can go next door, though."

Doughnut nickered, almost like he was reassuring her that her parents would be okay here alone for a few days. Nicole's nerves reappeared, but they quickly evaporated again.

It was simply very hard to feel like the weight of the world mattered out here, almost like this ranch didn't experience the same gravity as everywhere else.

"Yeah." She patted the horse again and added, "But I'm really nervous about singing in the Christmas program. Like, really nervous."

She'd looked through the music, and it wasn't too far from the standard stuff. A couple of rearrangements that she'd already memorized. She'd been singing them in the shower, the only place she really allowed herself to sing.

The humming and low vocalizations around the

animal hospital were nothing to what she could actually do, and out here on the ranch, she actually felt confident enough that she could sing in front of people.

Well, maybe just this horse. She pushed out all of her breath and took in a new one. Then she opened her mouth and started singing.

Chapter Seventeen

"And you know, I just don't know what to do to help her." Boone finished talking to Juniper, his new riding companion. He missed Peony, but Juniper was a good horse too. One of Squire's favorites, and one they'd just moved over from the ranch to the therapy operation.

Juniper didn't say anything, just lifted her head as she smelled something tasty. Boone let her wander toward a fresh patch of grass, as they weren't contained by fences or gates. Just the way he liked it.

He breathed in and then out, wishing he could find the peace out here that he so often had.

But Nicole's nerves seemed to have infected him too. He did want to help her with her stage fright, because she had a truly beautiful voice.

He didn't want to push her too hard, though, because while she put on a tough front of helping her parents, staying in Three Rivers her whole life, and running the animal hospital, he'd learned she was fragile underneath.

He supposed he was too, and as they'd gotten to know each other and shared their pasts and presents and hopes for the future with one another, he'd realized that.

"I really like her," he whispered to Juniper. "I'm not sure how to make sure she knows that either."

His mind went round and round, this therapy session one that wouldn't be resolved in a single hour. Which was fine. Boone had used an entire month of sessions to figure out if he even wanted to stay in Three Rivers.

Funny how now he never wanted to leave.

The peace came then, and Boone had at least one answer to a question that had been plaguing him. He hadn't told Cash Drew that he was out completely, but now he knew he needed to.

He dismounted, wanting to take a few extra minutes to get back to the stable, and started walking with Juniper's reins held loosely in his hand. "Come on, girl," he said as if the horse wasn't already coming.

He'd grown up a cowboy and had resisted almost everything about it—except his love of dogs and horses. The animals. It always came back to them.

As he approached the fenced pasture just outside the barn, a beautiful voice lifted into the air. He paused and looked up, easily finding Nicole atop Doughnut. They were magnificent together, and her face radiated pure joy as she sang about the Savior's birth.

Something stirred inside Boone that hadn't in a very long time. Yes, he'd been going back to church and actually enjoying it. His tongue didn't trip over prayers anymore.

But this was different. This was something he hadn't expected to feel for a woman, maybe ever. It felt like love, and Boone's heart flipped and flopped around in his chest as if trying to understand.

Nicole finished singing, a smile on her face, and leaned over to pat her horse. Boone got moving again, deciding on the spot that if she asked if he'd heard he singing, he'd deny it to the end of his days.

Or at least until they were married.

He stumbled, shock traveling through him and making his feet slow.

"Boone?" Nicole called, and his gaze shot toward her. He managed to lift his hand in greeting, but he continued toward the stable.

That word—*marriage*—circled in his mind as he brushed down Juniper and made small talk with Bennett and waited for Nicole to finish up. He sorely needed a drink if he was going to talk to Nicole on the drive home, so he ducked into the main building for Courage Reins and gulped greedily from the drinking fountain.

"You okay?" Reese asked, appearing in the hallway.

"Yeah." Boone straightened and wiped his mouth. "Yeah, I'm okay." But he scheduled another appointment for the following weekend instead of skipping a week like he'd been doing. Thankfully, Reese didn't ask why.

* * *

Boone and Nicole settled into a routine. She made the sixteen-step journey to his office every morning when he arrived to collect the coffee he'd brought for her. Her mind had somehow been changed, and she didn't feel the need to keep up the personal rules at work.

So she kissed Boone in his office in the morning, or whenever she passed and he happened to be in there alone. He brought her the chicken chop salad every Tuesday, and when they stayed late together on Thursday nights, Boone thought only heaven could be better.

Halloween came and went, and they dressed up like Frankenstein and the Bride of Frankenstein. It was probably the perfect time for Boone to ask Nicole about getting married, start to see how she felt about that, but he didn't.

She didn't bring it up either, which was a pretty big indicator for him that she wasn't quite ready. He wondered if she'd ever dreamed about her own wedding, in that gorgeous backyard of hers.

As Thanksgiving approached, his texts to his mother increased. Or rather, her texts to him. She wanted to know everything about Nicole, from what she looked like to what kind of pie she liked.

Boone, not the greatest texter on the planet, gave her what she asked for in short sentences.

It's pie, Mom. Who doesn't like pie?

Well, do you know what kind?

No, let me go ask.

He made the sixteen step journey to Nicole's office and leaned in the doorway. "My mother would like to know what kind of pie you like."

Nicole glanced away from her computer, a glazed look in her eye. "Pie?"

"Pie." He sighed like his mother was being difficult on purpose. But deep down, he loved that she was excited for him and wanted to make Thanksgiving special for him and Nicole.

"Pumpkin, I guess. Pecan for sure."

"I'll tell her." He pulled out his phone and sent the message, saying, "Are we set to leave on Tuesday after work?"

Only four more days. A measure of exhaustion pulled through him at the thought of driving to Grape Seed Falls and facing his family. But with Nicole at his side, he could do it. He'd be on his best behavior, and his mother had promised everyone there would be too.

"Yes," Nicole said. "I've got everything arranged for my parents. Shirley Bates will check on Mama in the evenings, and she has my number. Valcor and Tax are going to Dylan's. And...."

Boone glanced up from his phone, sensing some trepidation in his girlfriend. He stepped all the way into her office and sat down across from her. "And?"

"And I'm ready," she said, squaring her shoulders. "You promised me a tour of Hill Country, and you better not disappoint." She grinned at him, the sparkle in her eyes so lovely Boone laughed.

"It's going to be great," he said. "I've got the perfect place for us on Tuesday night, and then we'll continue to Grape Seed Falls on Wednesday. I've mapped out all the best places to stop and wander a little, and I found a great place for lunch that day."

"I can't wait."

Boone stood as the alarm on his phone went off. "Oh, I have a surgery I need to prep for." He headed for the door, turning back before he left. "And Nicole, I can't wait either."

He was definitely going to talk to her about marriage at some point this weekend. He was. He definitely was.

Tuesday seemed to arrive in the blink of an eye. He and Nicole worked most of the day in the hospital, as they'd planned to leave at three o'clock.

But as the time moved to that and beyond, Nicole was still rushing around, double-checking with the employees that were staying in town about the orphaned cats and dogs and their care, as well as one little pup that had had surgery that morning and still hadn't been picked up.

Boone's stomach turned as he watched her, because while he believed she wanted to go on this trip with him, he also knew it was hard for her.

She finally met him in the lobby closer to four than three and said, "I'm so sorry. I thought everything was ready."

"It's fine." He stood and ran his hands from hers to her shoulders and back, taking her fingers between his. "You're okay? You still want to go?"

She looked up at him, her expression softening by the moment. "Of course I want to go. I have my bags in the front room at home. You're following me?"

"Yeah, let's go." He did follow her to her house, loaded up her bags, and then drove her and her dogs to Dylan's apartment.

"Vader and Leia are at my place," he said. "You're still good to go get them later?"

"Sure thing." Dylan looked back and forth between Nicole, who was kneeling as she cooed to her tiny poodle, and Boone. "You two have fun." He grinned in a way Boone didn't entirely appreciate and handed him an envelope.

"What's this?"

"Read it on the way out," he said.

Boone shoved the envelope in his back pocket, annoyed that he'd have to read something non-work related. Maybe he could have Nicole read whatever it was.

She returned to his side, and he put his arm around her. "All right. Thanks, Dylan."

They left, and as Boone drove his truck outside the city limits of Three Rivers, all the tension left his body. "We're on our way, sweetheart," he said, the excitement that had kept him awake the past couple of nights finally returning.

She looked over at him, a wide smile on her face, and said, "We sure are."

He pulled the envelope out of his pocket and handed it to her. "Dylan gave me this. Will you read it to me?"

She gave him a curious look but took the envelope and pulled out a newspaper clipping. "It's by Gentry Pace, and it's about the animal hospital." She cleared her throat and read, "The City Council has approved the following items for discussion on next week's agenda: the road conditions on the southeast side of town and the proposition for a new building for the Puppy Pawz Animal Hospital."

"A *new* building?" Boone frowned. "I didn't submit anything to the City Council, and I rent that building." He glanced at the paper, but when Nicole tipped it toward him and pointed, the article was very short and there was no way he could read it.

"What else does it say?" He'd been all for raising public concern for the building if *the city* was going to foot the bill to update it. But if he had to?

"It says a concerned citizen has petitioned for the animal hospital to be relocated and that all parties will be notified before the meeting next week."

"I should be notified, don't you think?" he said. "Do you think we have an upset client?" He looked at Nicole, the two-lane highway they drove down pretty empty. "Has our building been a problem?"

In his eyes, it wasn't. Sure, sometimes the air conditioning went out for an hour or so, but Nicole made a call and someone came and fixed it. Problem solved.

Boone liked the building his animal hospital was in—he could afford the rent. A newer, nicer building might be out of his budget, and he suddenly wished he hadn't told Cash that he was out for the clinic in Amarillo.

He felt trapped, and he worked to breathe in and out.

"I don't know of anyone who's upset," Nicole said. "I'm sure it'll be fine."

Boone grunted, because he wasn't so sure. The first article Dylan had showed him had been months ago, so whoever was concerned about Puppy Pawz wasn't going to just disappear.

"Look at that!" Nicole pointed to a herd of animals out her window. "Are those...buffalo?"

Boone looked, and sure enough, the domesticated buffalo herd had migrated close to the highway today. "Yeah," he said, diving into the story of how the buffalo had come to be there.

Before he knew it, his tension had gone and he and Nicole talked the whole way to Llano. "It's only another half-hour to Grape Seed Falls," he said as he pulled into the parking lot at the B&B where they were staying. "But we'll go over to Horseshoe Falls and Kingsland and all that tomorrow."

He peered out the window at the beautiful, two-story home in front of them, which was lit with Christmas lights already. "This is where we're staying tonight. The Blue-bonnet Bed and Breakfast."

Nicole's fingers twined through his, though it was dark and she surely couldn't see much more than the house. "It's wonderful. Thank you, Boone."

He looked at her, his courage high and his desire for her raging through him like river rapids. "Nicole, I wanted to ask you about something."

"All right."

His grip on her hand tightened, almost like he thought she'd bolt if he said the wrong thing. "I'm wondering how you feel about marriage. About us—" He cleared his throat. "Getting married."

Chapter Eighteen

Nicole's eyes rounded and her breath caught in her chest. No matter how hard she tried to breathe in or out, it wasn't happening.

"I mean, not right away or anything," Boone added hastily. "I just thought maybe we'd start talking about it."

Marriage.

"You want to get married?" she asked, her voice more of a squeak than anything else.

Boone's eyes searched hers, and with only the multi-colored light from the house in front of them, she couldn't quite decipher what emotions he was feeling.

"If you're not ready to talk about this, it's fine." He looked away, the air between them charged now when it had been fun and light and playful for the last several hours.

"I don't know what I'm ready to talk about." Nicole felt like someone had put her on a pottery wheel and had just started spinning, and spinning, and spinning.

Shaping, and pressing, and twisting.

Was Boone in love with her? Did she love him?

Would her parents be okay while she was gone?

Would his parents like her?

"I'm experiencing a lot of new things right now," she continued, a prayer starting in her heart that he would understand, that she wouldn't hurt his feelings.

"Yeah, I know."

"So let's go inside," she said. "And maybe we can talk about this in the morning?"

"Sure." Boone didn't look at her as he got out and helped her down. He collected all their luggage from the back of his truck and he led the way inside to check in. He'd taken care of everything—including her—and a rush of affection hit her hard.

And dang, if breathing wasn't hard again. Because she really liked Boone—*did she love him?*—and found him strong and rugged and sexier than any man she'd ever known.

Not that there were a lot of those, but still. She'd had no idea she could have a man like him in her life, and part of her still wondered what in the world he was doing with her.

Plain old Nicole. Overlooked and thought about last.

But with Boone, he seemed to think about her before himself, and she had no idea what to do with that.

"You're in the Little Acorn room," he said, handing her a key. "It's on the second floor in the corner." He started for the stairs, all the luggage in tow.

"Where are you?" she asked.

"Um, Timber Rose? It's in the opposite corner." He left his luggage at the top of the stairs and continued down the hall to her room. He waited while she fitted her key in the lock and went inside.

After he'd pushed her suitcases in, he lingered in the doorway while she admired the huge king bed and the fireplace across from it.

"All right," he finally said, and Nicole turned to face him. "We can get up whenever. It's been a long day, so if you want to sleep in, go ahead." He ran his fingers through his hair, almost a nervous gesture, and took a step backward.

Nicole took a step into him, wrapping her arms around him and leaning her cheek against his pulse. "Thank you, Boone," she said, her voice barley loud enough to reach her own ears. "This is wonderful." She looked up at him. "*You're* wonderful."

He gazed down on her and with these brighter lights, she could definitely see some hints of love in his eyes. "See you in the morning." He bent down and kissed her, a magical kiss that was filled with tender emotion. She wanted it to last forever, but he broke their connection and left her room.

She leaned in the doorway and watched him collect his bag and continue to the room at the far end of the hall, same side as hers. A sigh passed through her body, and Nicole knew in that moment that she absolutely was ready to discuss marriage with Boone Carver.

NICOLE WOKE with the sun the next morning, and while it was a bit later now that it was later in the year, it certainly couldn't be counted as sleeping in.

She showered with soap scented with lavender and admired the view out the front of the house. She imagined what the fields of flowers would look like in the spring when the bluebonnets bloomed, and she hugged herself as a smile touched her mouth.

A man came jogging down the road, and she recognized the strong gait as Boone's instantly. A giggle left her mouth, because only Boone would get up early and get his running in.

Of course, the marathon was only a couple of months away now, and he couldn't let up on his training regimen just because it was the holidays.

She watched him slow to a walk and go through his cool down routine, rather enjoying the show. He didn't seem troubled, and that helped her feel better about their non-conversation about marriage last night.

When he started toward the front door, she left her room so she'd "accidentally" bump into him on the stairs.

"Oh, hey," she said as if she hadn't expected to see him coming up while she went down. She beamed up at him and let him take her into his arms.

"I'm sweaty," he said, just the slightest puff still in his breathing.

"How many miles this morning?" she asked.

"Just eleven."

"Oh, only eleven. What a ridiculously low amount." She felt like her grin would crack her face.

He laughed and said, "Give me twenty minutes to shower. Then we can eat and go."

"All right."

He released her and continued upstairs, those shorts absolutely criminal. Nicole fanned herself as she finished descending the steps, though it was nowhere near hot enough to be as flushed as she was.

Once they'd eaten, loaded up their bags, and set the truck more east than south, Nicole said, "I think it's probably a good time for us to talk about marriage."

Boone jerked the wheel as he looked at her. "Yeah?" He steadied the truck back into his own lane.

"Yeah," she said. "I mean, what does that look like for you?"

"Well, I—" He blew out his breath. "I don't know. I think the bride plans most of it."

"I'd like it to be in my backyard," Nicole said. "Friends and family. A full dinner."

"So you've thought about getting married," he said, slipping his hand into hers.

"Not a lot," she admitted. "Remember how I didn't date before you?"

"I remember." He lifted her wrist to his lips. "And it sounds great to get married in your backyard. I'm assuming summertime?"

"*This* summer?"

"I don't know, Nicole." He spoke with a measure of reverence in his voice, and she liked it when he said her name with such softness and seriousness.

"Okay, but yes," she said. "The yard is definitely at it's best in the summer. Early fall, actually."

"Early fall," he echoed, his attention out the windshield absolute. Only minutes later, they turned off the highway toward Buchanan Dam.

"All right," he said. "Now this is one of my favorite places. My dad used to bring us up here to fish and swim."

The rest of the day was spent with him introducing her to his Memory Lane and her experiencing the beauty of Texas Hill Country.

They ate lunch at a quaint shop that only sold barbecue, and while Nicole was a native Texan, she had never had ribs that flavorful before.

"All right," Boone drawled, somehow making his accent twice as strong as she'd ever heard it. "Next stop: Grape Seed Falls Ranch."

He put the truck in gear and they left behind Lake Marble Falls and headed toward Johnson City and Grape Seed Falls according to the sign.

"Are you nervous?" she asked, her own stomach already rioting quite fiercely.

"Yes," he admitted. "I've never brought anyone home before, and yeah." He shrugged. "I'm nervous."

"Tell me their names again." He'd been telling her for weeks, and Nicole already knew, but she liked listening to him—plus, she'd learned that if she could keep him talking, he became less anxious.

"Dwayne is married to Felicity," he said. "And Heather and Levi are engaged and getting married just after Christmas. I suppose I'll have to come back for that."

"And you're just now thinking of that?" she asked.

"I didn't want to commit, in case this...you know. Goes badly."

"She's your sister."

"Yeah, I know."

"You talk to her," Nicole said. "You're definitely going to her wedding."

He made a turn and didn't answer. In fact, anything else she tried to say to him, he just nodded or shook his head until he said, "There it is."

He turned again and went under an arch that had

peaches carved into it. "Here we go." His phone buzzed, and he slowed the truck to a crawl to check it.

"My brother just texted to say they're down in the Cabin Community," he said, his own nerves a palpable scent on the air. "They've invited the whole crew to meet us." He glanced at her. "All the cowboys, Nicole."

"It's going to be great," Nicole said with a forced amount of enthusiasm in her voice.

"I haven't seen them in a while," he said, almost like a confession. He eased the truck past the homestead and on down a different road, toward another stand of buildings and big, tall flagpole.

Smoke lifted from somewhere nearby that pole, and it wasn't until he rounded the corner where the barn stood that she saw all the people. Every man wore a cowboy hat, and there were a lot of them. Easily twenty people sat at long tables covered in white paper, and her own nerves urged her to stay in the truck.

"It's going to be fine," she repeated as he parked down the road a bit as there wasn't much space by the grassy area where everyone had congregated.

She peered out the windshield, same as him, wondering what was so awful about his family that he didn't go visit them. "Let's go, Boone. It'll be fine." She unbuckled her seatbelt but didn't get out of the vehicle. "Brother's name is Dwayne. He's two years older than you and runs your family's ranch. Wife is Felicity. Your sister is Heather, and she's two years younger than you and teaches third grade. Levi is her fiancé. Your parents are Maggie and Chase Carver."

She smiled at her own memory and glanced at him. His face was a mask. "Right? Boone? Did I get it right?"

"Yeah, that's right." He opened the door and the scent of roasted and smoked meats increased, along with the tangy quality of barbecue sauce. Nicole's mouth watered, and she realized she hadn't really enjoyed Texas barbecue until this road trip.

As they approached hand-in-hand, a woman with beautiful light brown—almost blonde—hair stood. She was clearly Boone's mother, what with those high cheekbones and fiery eyes. She didn't look at her son for very long, but kept her blue-gray eyes on Nicole. She stumbled around the chairs in her way and flew toward them.

"Boone." Her voice caught. "Look at you." She stretched up to hug him and he easily embraced her, his eyes pressing closed for several long heartbeats.

"Hey, Ma." He cleared his throat of the obvious emotion there and stepped back. "This is Nicole Hymas."

His mother couldn't speak as the tears fell down her face. She grabbed onto Nicole and held her close too, whispering, "It's so great to meet you."

Warmth and acceptance filled Nicole, and she smiled at Boone's mom. "Nice to meet you too, ma'am."

Boone moved through the crowd, hugging a man that looked remarkably like him, and laughing and talking with another woman and the man who had his arm around her.

He didn't cry, but whatever he'd been worried about didn't seem to exist. His father looked proud and happy; his brother could only smile; his sister held his hand while they went through the line to get introductions.

Nicole didn't quite know where she fit in this Carver family reunion, but she was happy to stand to the side and smile, like she'd done for so many years of her life. He clearly belonged to them, and they'd clearly let him go but not cut him off.

He'd told her that his father disapproved of his choice to leave the ranch and that they argued a lot, but Nicole couldn't detect any ill will in the man at all.

Maybe it was all the people around them. She met a dozen cowboys whose names she'd never remember and then Dwayne swept her into a hug with the words, "I never thought Boone could get someone to marry him."

"Hey," Boone said. "Look who's talking."

Nicole smiled, unsure of what to say. Dwayne acted like Boone was the lucky one. Everyone was looking at her like that, and she really didn't know what to do with this type of spotlight.

"Let's eat," his father said. "I'm starving." He swept the crowd and his eyes landed on Boone, who stood several paces away from Nicole. "Boone, will you say grace?"

It was if the group sucked in a collective breath, and Heather stepped forward and said, "Dad, I can—"

"Sure," Boone said over her. "I'd love to."

Nicole's eyes flew back to his dad, and he clearly

looked like someone had tossed ice water in his face. But he folded his arms as his eyes narrowed, and Nicole suddenly understood the passive, quiet animosity Boone had tried to describe to her.

She barely heard Boone's prayer over the food, as she was busy pleading with the Lord to make this visit pleasant for Boone in every way possible.

Chapter Nineteen

"He's not overbearing," Nicole said as Boone walked through the door. His heart jumped. He knew he shouldn't have left Nicole alone with his parents and Heather, even if he had been interested in Dwayne's new horse.

Thanksgiving Day had been beautiful, with a plenty of food and gratitude and good cheer. But it was Friday now, and apparently his family thought all bets were off and they could ask whatever they wanted.

Boone paused before entering the kitchen, not wanting to eavesdrop but needing to know what they were asking her.

"Well, that's good," his dad said. "Sometimes Boone likes to fix things that are unfixable."

What did that even mean? There was nothing to fix with Nicole anyway.

"Chase," his mother said, and Boone suspected his mother knew he'd come in. He got himself around the corner and into the kitchen.

"What did I miss?" he asked.

"Nothing," Nicole said, stepping over to him with definite anxiety in her expression. He put his arm around her and wanted to lead her out to the truck and on out of Hill Country.

"We were just asking Nicole about how you guys met and started dating," Heather said. She too wore a hint of nervousness on her face, and Boone really disliked that his father had that affect on everyone and didn't seem to notice or care.

"Oh," Boone said. "Did she tell you about my running shorts?"

"It came up," Heather said lightly, and Nicole started laughing.

"Thanks for that," Boone growled in her ear, flashing her a smile so she'd know he wasn't really upset, and he said loud enough for everyone to hear, "Well, we're going to head back into town."

"So soon?" His mom stepped around the counter. "There's still cookies and ice cream."

"I'm stuffed, Mom," he said, not wanting to hurt her feelings but not wanting to hang around the ranch any longer. This visit had definitely been one of the best he'd had, but his father hadn't changed all that much.

"All right," she said. "I can box you some for the drive tomorrow?"

"Sure." He waited while she did that, and then he nudged Nicole toward the door. Heather and his mother talked in the kitchen, a binder open on the counter between them as Heather went over her forthcoming wedding plans.

"Boone, can I have a moment?" His father had a way of appearing right when Boone thought he could make a clean getaway.

"Sure. You go on ahead, Nicole." He handed her the keys to his truck though she wore an expression that said she didn't want to leave him alone.

He smiled at her, and she went through the front door, and Boone sat on the couch in the living room, waiting for his father to say whatever it was he felt like he needed to say.

He sat down with a sigh and said, "She seems nice."

"She is," Boone said. He had not mentioned their brief marriage conversation. His mother had already cried at the fact that he even had a girlfriend. He didn't need to go getting her hopes up.

"Are you sure she's not...beneath you?" His dad wore a look of genuine concern.

"I don't even know what that means, Dad."

"I just want what's best for you."

Boone stood, the conversation already stale. He'd heard all of this before. "Dad, you have no idea what would make me happy." He started for the front door and opened it. "Ranching didn't do it, and you think I settled for a career in veterinary medicine."

He spun back to his dad, who had also stood. "But I didn't. I'm good at what I do, and I love it. And I love her too. She's not beneath me. If anything, she's out of my league."

His chest hurt, and his mother appeared at the mouth of the hallway, followed by Heather. "Good-bye, Mother." He looked at his sister, unwilling to break her heart but needed to preserve his too. "I don't know if I'll make it to the wedding, Heather. I'll let you know."

With his attention then on his father, Boone said, "'Bye, Dad. Take care."

"Boone," his mom said, but Boone held up his hand. He turned and left the house, almost running straight into Nicole.

"Come on," he said, almost brushing past her when he wanted to grab onto her and anchor himself. His anger boiled along with his father's words

He wasn't sure why his mind seized onto them when he should let them go, but they did. *Are you sure she's not beneath you?*

Why did his father think he was anything special? If anything, his dad had spent the better part of Boone's adult life disapproving of everything he did.

"Did I hear you say...? Never mind."

"What?" Boone snapped, realizing too late his mistake.

"I"m sorry, Nicole," he said, his anger softening but not going away. "I'm—my father is impossible."

"He seems to love you," she said carefully.

"Oh, yeah? Is that what you'd call it?" Was she seriously going to side with his dad?

"But at the same time, he takes little digs at you. He wanted to know if you'd 'interfered' in my life yet."

Boone slammed on the brakes and twisted to look at her. *"Interfered?"* His fury roared, and Boone's jaw clenched so hard his bones ached. "That's just...." He peered at her. "Have I?"

"Boone, of course not." Nicole reached up and cradled his face in her hand. He tried to seize onto the comfort her touch had always brought him, but it was slippery and he couldn't quite do it.

"Let's go home," she said, and Boone liked that idea best out of any he'd had recently. So he set the truck north and barely looked in his rear view mirror.

By the time they rolled up to her place in the older part of Three Rivers, Boone's anger had simmered out.

"Your mother has messaged you a number of times," Nicole said, indicating his phone on the dashboard.

"I know.

"Are you going to call her?"

"Not tonight," he said, looking at Nicole. The tension between them felt unfair, and Boone got out of the truck to get her bags down for her. "I'll bring your dogs back in the morning, okay?"

"Okay." She stretched up and kissed him, and Boone watched her walk inside and close the door behind her before he turned to get behind the wheel again.

Courage Reins wouldn't be open as late as it was, but Boone couldn't wait to get out there in the morning. He had a lot to tell Juniper and he didn't think he'd get much sleep tonight as his father's words and Boone's questions continued to rotate in his mind.

* * *

BOONE VISITED with Juniper twice before he sat down to Tuesday evening's City Council meeting. He had indeed been informed of the concern over the building's safety for humans and pets alike, and the name on the letter had been a law office in town.

He'd called the number and found out that the person responsible for the whole situation was Penelope Whitby. He didn't know her, and Nicole hadn't been able to find her or any name like hers in their client files.

Nicole sat beside him, and he held her hand as a way to keep himself calm. The meeting started, and Boone learned why he'd never want to be a politician or a public servant as it seemed nothing was talked about and then voted on.

An hour in, the topic of the animal shelter building hit the table, and Boone perked up. A petite blonde woman stood at the microphone and started speaking about the heating and air conditioning issues, and Nicole leaned over.

"That's Penny *Welch*," she said. "She used to work at the animal hospital."

Boone kept his eyes on her. "She did?" He'd never seen her before, and he would've remembered heels that high.

"Yeah, Doctor Von fired her a couple of years ago. I'd heard she'd moved and gotten married, but apparently, she's back."

"...and that building is unfit for animals to live in full-time," Penelope said. "The animal hospital should be updated or relocated. It's inhumane otherwise."

"Why does she care?" Boone tried to get a better look at the woman's face, but she seemed to know he wanted to see her and she kept her eyes straight forward on the City Council members.

"I don't know." Nicole straightened and when Penelope finished, Boone stood.

He slicked his palms down the front of his slacks, glad he dressed up for work each day. "Hello," he said into the microphone. "I'm Boone Carver, and I own and operate Puppy Pawz."

"You've read the complaints by Miss Whitby?"

"Excuse me," Penelope said, standing from her chair only a step away from the microphone. "It's *Mrs.* Whitby. I'm married to Doctor Louis Whitby."

Boone gaped at her, the name tickling some old

memory in the back of his mind. He'd known a Louis Whitby in veterinarian school, and the man hadn't passed several exams and dropped out for a semester to study some more.

Boone had moved on and never heard from or seen the man again. *What a small world that he'd be in Three Rivers*, Boone thought.

"You've read the complaints by Mrs. Whitby?" the City Council member said again, a definite measure of exasperation in his voice.

"Yes." Boone faced the front of the room again, wondering why Louis wanted to shut down his clinic. "And as the city owns the building and I simply rent it, I'd love to see this Council approve a budget for repairs on the building."

He took a breath and sent a prayer heavenward before he spoke again. "But rest assured that the staff and animals at Puppy Pawz are perfectly safe. The pipes are not leaking, as *Mrs.* Whitby claims. I would know; I work in the building every day of the week. She hasn't stepped foot in my clinic since I've been here, and that's been over a year."

"I'm afraid we don't have anything in the budget for this year," the councilman said.

"The air conditioning sometimes goes out, and my office administrator calls immediately and gets it fixed. There is no suffering going on at the animal hospital." He shot Penelope a defiant glare, and she glared right back.

"So we can table this discussion for now," the councilman said, looking down his row. "Do we want to vote on that?"

"Perhaps we should do an investigation," a woman beside him said. "See if the claims have any merit."

"Who's for that?" the councilman asked, and every hand at the front of the room went up. He faced Boone again. "We'll contract with someone who can make an honest and fair assessment on the conditions at the animal hospital and be in touch."

Boone nodded, not exactly the outcome he wanted, and walked back to his seat. At least they hadn't shut down his clinic or ordered him to find a more expensive building.

"We need to find out everything we can about Louis and Penelope Whitby," he muttered to Nicole, only mildly satisfied when she said, "I'll get on that first thing tomorrow."

It seemed everything and everyone was against him at the moment, as Heather hadn't been pleased when Boone had confirmed he would not be returning to Hill Country for her December twenty-eighth wedding. Even his mother's pleas had not swayed him.

And now this.

As he left the meeting with Nicole's hand in his, he thought *At least I have her.*

Chapter Twenty

And I love her too.

Nicole had definitely heard Boone say that after he'd opened his parents' front door.

She had no idea what to do with the words, and she didn't dare ask him about them. They'd started talking about getting married, and she should've known his feelings for her were that strong.

It was just so...*unbelievable.*

She sighed and clicked to another website, having spent a couple of hours on the Internet that morning already, as Boone spent Wednesdays out at the ranch. Joanne did vaccinations and handled the pet daycare, leaving Nicole in peace.

She couldn't figure out why the Whitby's cared what was happening within the walls at Puppy Pawz. Penelope had grown up here and worked at the clinic under Dr.

Von. She'd made several comments to clients that upset them, and the vet had asked her to leave.

She had. No questions. No fuss. She really wasn't a people person, and the receptionist job hadn't been a good fit for her. She's married Louis later that year, and they'd moved further south.

They were apparently back in Three Rivers, and had been for about five months. According to what Nicole could learn, her husband didn't have a job and neither did Penny.

Nicole sat back and looked at her notes. "Maybe she wants to drive Boone out of town," she said. "Then her husband can buy the clinic."

It was the best she had, and she texted the information and her speculations to Boone before lunch. He didn't respond until evening, when she was walking into the church for choir practice.

Thanks, sweetheart. See you after choir?

Sure, she sent, instantly warm at his term of endearment, and stuffed her phone in her purse. With only a few weeks until Christmas, Nicole was going to have to figure out how to sing in front of people.

Brother Myron had been very kind, saying things like, "This is where Nicole will sing her solo," and moving on during practices. She didn't mind singing with the thirty or so members in the choir, but she didn't want to belt out a tune *in front* of them.

And when there were people sitting in the pews?

Nicole shivered just thinking about it.

Every song in her head in the mornings were the Christmas tunes she'd be singing during the program. She did practice her parts—at home, without spectators.

She just needed to find the courage to open her mouth and sing when it was the right time.

"Let's go over Joy to the World," Brother Myron said after they'd said an opening prayer for the practice. He faced her. "Nicole, are you ready to sing for us?"

He asked her this every week, and all she had to do was shake her head yes or no. Everyone looked at her, and she glanced down the row at them. "I'll try," she said, feeling stronger and more brave than she ever had.

Brother Myron grinned and he indicated the pianist should begin playing. She wasn't singing her solo until the third verse, and she didn't open her mouth to sing during the first two either.

She just let the spirit of the song flow through her, her stomach growing more and more cramped as her time to sing approached.

When the moment arrived, Nicole opened her mouth and sang. It wasn't very good, and there was no way anyone past the third row would be able to hear her, but she did it.

Brother Myron grinned like she'd just solved world peace and when the song ended, he engulfed her in a giant hug. "That was great, Nicole," he said. "Maybe just a little louder next time."

He moved seamlessly onto the next song, and Nicole appreciated the beefy older gentleman more than she ever had. She looked at the woman standing next to her, and Andy patted her hand. "Good job, Nicole."

But Nicole knew it was not a good job. Not worthy of being a soloist, and Andy definitely knew it too.

She didn't sing again during the practice, and when she got home, she didn't call Boone either.

Maybe you like being overlooked, she thought as she heated something to eat in the microwave. And she had no argument for that.

* * *

CHRISTMAS APPROACHED no matter what Nicole did. She attended every choir practice; knew all the songs by heart; woke with more than one song in her head for the day because of how often she thought about the Christmas program.

Boone assured her and reassured her that the town of Three Rivers wouldn't know what hit it once the Christmas program ended, and he'd even suggested she try to get Mama to come to the service. "At least for ten minutes," he said.

Nicole hadn't known how that was possible, but Boone worked everything out with her dad, and Mama was coming.

Nicole had been toying with the idea of inviting her

siblings. At least the two who lived in the continental United States. In the end, she didn't, still not sure why forgiving them seemed to be taking so long.

"You ready?" Boone asked as she entered her office the Friday before the performance. He'd arrived ahead of her at Puppy Pawz and was already coated up for the day.

"Are you ready for the marathon?" She glared at him until he stood from her chair behind the desk.

"Okay, so we're not in a good mood this morning." He nudged the coffee he brought for her every morning. "We'll talk after you're properly caffeinated." He left in a hurry, and Nicole didn't blame him. She sipped the coffee, but it made her already boiling stomach worse. What had she been thinking? How could she possibly get up in front of *everyone* and sing?

Singing for Boone had been horrible, every nerve standing at attention. When she'd first started practicing with the choir, she'd almost thrown up beforehand. The only reason she hadn't was because Brother Myron had found her in the parking lot and told her she didn't have to sing during practices if she didn't want to.

But now....

You have to sing, she thought.

"I can't do it." She reached for her phone, an overwhelming desire to leave town and never come back surging through her. She had Pastor Scott dialed before her brain kicked against her panic. She hung up, her palms slick and her pulse ragged.

Somehow, the day passed. Saturday too. Sunday came, and she stood in her house, fingering the navy blue choir robes she'd wear in just a few short hours. She'd confessed all her fears to Boone, and he'd comforted her for at least the fiftieth time. He must be so sick of her by now, and Nicole couldn't wait until the Christmas program was over.

She only hoped her relationship wouldn't be.

Over the months, Boone had taken to sitting with her on the third row, and today was no different. She arrived only moments before the service began and slid onto the bench next to him.

"Didn't think you were coming," he said.

"I almost didn't."

"I called you three times. I was about to drive over and get you myself."

"Been out walking."

He peered at her, ultimate concern on his face. "Isn't it raining?"

"Not much." She stared straight forward, her stomach so tight and not getting any looser. The walk hadn't helped. Eating hadn't helped. Getting Mama ready to leave the house hadn't helped.

Even sitting next to Boone wasn't helping. The service started and Pastor Scott said a few things after the opening prayer. Then the dreaded words, "We'll now turn the rest of our time over to the choir for their musical performance to represent the birth of the Savior," were said, and the other choir members rose from the congregation.

Nicole couldn't seem to get her feet moving before Andy paused at the end of the aisle and stared at her pointedly. Nicole got up. Got herself to the choir chairs and in position next to Andy. She even managed a tight smile at the woman, who patted her arm and gave her a reassuring smile.

But Nicole didn't want to be touched right now. She almost yanked her arm away. The band started and the choir belted out its first song. Nicole mouthed along to *Joy to the World*, wishing she could find the Christmas spirit to help her through the next forty-five minutes.

The third verse came. Her time to sing. She stood there mute. The congregation blurred—all except one face.

Boone's face.

He watched her intently, his eyes hopeful but his mouth tense. The band cycled through the intro again, and still Nicole couldn't seem to emit much more than a squeak. Horror poured through her and her stomach clenched tight, tighter, tightest.

She looked away from Boone, his presence completely unnerving her. On the third attempt, Nicole managed to get out the words, but the pitch was all over the place. Out of the corner of her eye, she caught sight of Boone making his way toward the choir seats.

She warned him back with a daggered glare, but he

kept on coming. He sidled next to her but wisely didn't touch her. Her hands started to shake and her voice matched them. The vibrato sounded terrible; the notes were all wrong. But she managed to finish the song.

Tears streamed down her face, and she turned away from Boone, though he was the closest escape. She pushed past the other choir members, ignoring Brother Myron's protests, and fled from the chapel, every eye focused on her.

She didn't hide out in the bathroom. She ran all the way to her car, her navy robes billowing behind her as her heels clicked against the blacktop.

"Nicole!" Boone called from behind her, but she didn't stop. Couldn't. She locked her car doors, jammed the key in the ignition, and tore out of the parking lot. Her eyes met Boone's for just a moment, but it was long enough to see his disappointment.

She cried as she set the sedan on the stretch of highway that would take her to Amarillo. She could do this drive; she'd done it before.

Interfere. Boone had interfered.

Overbearing. He *could* be overbearing, what with inviting her mother to watch Nicole's most embarrassing failure.

With every mile her tires ate, Nicole grew angrier and angrier. With herself. With God.

And with Boone Carver.

Chapter Twenty-One

Boone sat in his car until well past dark, his chest rioting with insects, then hummingbirds, then crows. He'd called Nicole ten times and texted her twice that. She hadn't responded once.

He'd done the same to his mother the day they'd left Grape Seed Falls, and pure regret filled him now. He even texted her an apology, though he'd already spoken to her and made things right.

He leaned back against the headrest, admitting to himself that he shouldn't have gone up to the choir seats. He just thought he could calm her enough to simply open her mouth and sing. She had, sort of. Her voice was nowhere near what he'd heard at his house, and now Nicole had disappeared.

Finally admitting defeat, he drove home, where Lord Vader and Princess Leia greeted him with wagging tails and slobbery kisses. He'd been neglecting his dogs in the evenings since he'd started dating Nicole six months ago, but they still seemed to love him.

"Come on, guys." He went down the hall to the master bedroom and changed into gym shorts and a T-shirt. He switched on the TV and fell into bed. He let Vader and Leia jump up and lay on either side of him, one hand stroking each dog. He needed them close right now, and he stole some comfort from them as the hours passed and his phone stayed silent.

THE FOLLOWING MORNING, he skipped his running for the day. Instead, he drove down the quiet, early-morning streets of Three Rivers at a crawl. Nothing had changed at Nicole's, which meant she hadn't come home last night. They'd made no plans for today, and the clinic wouldn't be open until Thursday. The sheltered animals still needed care, but Nicole had a schedule to make sure they got fed, watered, and exercised while the clinic was closed.

He didn't know the schedule, because he didn't need to know it, but he found himself pulling into the clinic. There weren't any other cars there, and he parked in the back like he usually did and entered the old building.

The familiar scent of cleaning supplies and animals met his nose, calming him for reasons he couldn't name. He'd slept poorly the previous night, his thoughts bouncing from Nicole to Puppy Pawz to the botched choir program.

At least his clinic had met the approval of the independent appraiser who'd come to see what the conditions were like. Penelope Whitby hadn't made a reappearance at any City Council meetings, and Boone hoped the whole affair would simply disappear.

Boone flipped on the lights and moved through the shelter, talking in a low voice to the animals. His phone went off, and he almost tripped over his own feet in his haste to pull it from his jacket pocket.

It wasn't Nicole, and his heart settled back into his heels. It was Brynn Greene, wondering if he could make a house call for one of her horses.

He responded that he'd be right out, and he retraced his steps and left the building. Sadness descended on him, and it felt like a heavy yoke around his neck. The past six months had been the best he'd had in Three Rivers, at Puppy Pawz. Now, he wondered if he'd ever be able to go back to that building and find anything worthwhile.

There was no way he could make that sixteen-step walk without his heart breaking. He'd told his father that he was in love with Nicole, and he'd marveled at that declaration since.

He hadn't told her yet. With all of her attention on the Christmas program, they hadn't even talked more about getting married.

He made it to the ranch, the beginnings of a migraine

starting behind his temples. He put on a smile and parked near the stables of Bowman's Breeds.

Nicole had come out to the equine therapy sessions with him for several weeks now, and he could barely get his feet to move toward the gate at the thought that they might never make the drive out here again.

He eradicated the thought. Surely she wouldn't break up with him because she hadn't been able to sing in church. *That* wasn't his fault, not by any stretch of the imagination. But the thought returned, and Boone had learned not to ignore his brain when it circled something. He texted her again.

Please let me know you're okay.

Simple. Not overbearing. He wasn't begging.

Brynn pushed through a door, a loud squeal coming with her and stealing his attention from his phone. "Hey, Brynn. Whaddya got?"

"Sunshine isn't doing great."

"She's the pregnant one?"

"I have about a dozen pregnant horses." Brynn threw him a look over her shoulder. "But she's one of 'em."

Boone followed her, not really in the mood to deal with a horse right now. Or another person. Or even himself. But he was a professional, and he did love his work out here at the ranch.

So he did his best to ignore the fact that his phone didn't chime or vibrate and put a smile on his face when

Brynn turned and gestured toward a stall where a beautiful gray and white horse should've been standing.

But Sunshine wasn't standing. She lay in the corner of the pen, her eyes a bit wild and her belly way too big. "How far along is she?" he asked, opening the gate and entering the pen.

Sunshine nickered at him, almost like a warning but not quite.

"Seven months," Brynn said. "Cal thinks it's twins."

"She needs to get up," Boone said, not sure why he thought that. But with two foals inside, she needed to be eating and drinking and staying on her feet. "How long has she been lying in the corner?"

"Since last night, I think," Brynn said. "I'm...Ethan came out and checked on the pregnant mares for me last night."

Boone glanced at her, everything he'd learned about Brynn in the past couple of years at odds with what she'd just said. She didn't let anyone do anything with her horses at Bowman's Breeds. *She* was the expert. *She* knew every little detail about every little thing.

She was very much like Nicole in that regard, and Boone's heart twisted once again.

"You didn't come out?" he asked.

She shook her head, her mouth pressed into a straight line. "I wasn't feeling well." She met his eye and added, "My morning sickness seems to hit me in the evenings. Go figure."

Boone blinked as he realized what she'd said. "Wow, congratulations, Brynn." He smiled at her, a real, genuine smile. He wasn't sure he could manage one of those at the moment, but he did.

"Thank you." She grinned, her whole being seeming to light up. "So I'm not sure. I texted Ethan about her this morning, and he said that yes, she was lying down last night too."

"And is that odd?"

"He didn't think so."

"What do you think?" Boone approached Sunshine, clicking his tongue at her. "What's wrong, girl? Too many babies in there?"

The likelihood that a mare could deliver more that one baby was pretty slim. If one of the fetuses had died, it could put the other one in danger. And delivering two healthy foals? It was the exception; Boone knew that much.

He put his hand on her neck, relieved when she let him. Her eyes drifted halfway closed, and a sense of peace entered Boone. It was amazing to him how calming a horse was, how his spirit simply quieted in their presence.

"Let me feel, okay?" He ran his fingertips down her neck and along her ribs, searching for the legs and feet of the baby. "Here's one here," he said, mostly for Brynn.

He watched Sunshine's face to make sure he wasn't causing her any pain. She wasn't panting. She didn't seem to be having a problem at all. And since he could only feel one side of her belly, he honestly didn't know if there was another foal inside or not.

"Let's get her bridled," he said. "Would you hand me what I need?"

Brynn complied, and Boone got Sunshine ready to stand. "All right, girl. Time to get up." He tugged on the reins, but she resisted. "Come on."

When the horse still didn't seem close to complying, he turned back to Brynn. "Maybe you should try."

A panicked look crossed her face, something Boone didn't understand. But she came into the stall and took the reins from him. "Ethan's concerned about me getting kicked," she said, and Boone supposed that made sense.

"Come on," she said to Sunshine. "Get up, Sunny."

The horse did for Brynn, stumbling the slightest bit until she settled her weight on all four legs.

"Keep her steady," Boon said, moving around the front of the horse to the other side. He pressed and felt, moving his hands slowly. "She's got some rot on this side," he said, brushing at her coat. "She can't lay down for that long."

Maybe Sunshine was just lazy.... "I don't think there's two babies in here either. You sure she'd only seven months along?"

"I think so."

Boone kept back his exasperated sigh. He wasn't sure why her non-answer bothered him so much. Probably because *everything* was bothering him today.

He prayed that he could find a well of patience he

didn't know about as he continued to probe for any sign of discomfort or distress with the horse.

"I don't think there's anything wrong with her," he finally said. "Make sure she's eating enough. Getting enough to drink. And she needs to exercise. She shouldn't be this big with just one foal."

"All right," Brynn said. "But Cal said—"

"I don't really care what Cal said." The words left Boone's mouth before he could censor them.

Brynn's gaze flew to his, and Boone apologized quickly. "I'm tired," he said. "Nicole—" He cut off, unable to continue. He brushed his hands off and moved out of the stall. "She's not talking to me at the moment. I'm a little...stressed."

Brynn's eyes softened, and she patted him on the shoulder like he was a dog. "She'll come around."

"I don't know why she's so upset."

"She's not used to being the center of attention." Brynn kept a grip on the reins and led the horse out of her stall. "Come on Sunshine. We have to keep walking. You can't be so lazy."

He simply closed the gate to the pen, followed her and Sunshine out, and headed home. But he didn't want to be there, so he leashed Vader and Leia and went to where he'd first *seen* Nicole for the first time.

Chapter Twenty-Two

Nicole spent the night in Amarillo at a hotel. In the past, she'd slept curled in a ball in her mother's hospital room. But she discovered this time that the city had charm, and the dreams she'd had about going to college and living in a big city brightened. She realized they'd never died. They'd simply taken up residence in the back of her mind.

Boone had called and texted dozens of times. She finally called him back near dinnertime on Monday, after she'd been gone for over twenty-four hours. He'd be furious with her, and she wouldn't blame him.

But she was also furious with him. He should never have pushed her to sing in church. Never left his seat to come up to the choir section. How humiliating. *Poor Nicole Hymas, forty years old and needs her boyfriend to help her sing a song.*

She shook her head, the angry tears pricking her eyes as the call finally connected.

"Nicole," Boone breathed into the line after only one ring. "Where are you? Are you okay? When are you coming home?"

He sounded desperate, frantic almost, and some of Nicole's anger cooled. "I'm in Amarillo. I'm fine. And I'll be home in time for work on Thursday." She honestly didn't know when she'd go back to Three Rivers. Could be tomorrow. Or Wednesday. Or maybe she'd get up early on Thursday morning and make the hour-long drive in barely enough time to arrive at her desk by nine-thirty. She wasn't sure.

"I've been to your mama's. She's doing okay."

Guilt gutted Nicole. She hadn't even thought about Mama and Daddy. "Thank you," ghosted from her mouth.

"I miss you," he said.

"I have to go." She hung up before he could say anything more. She didn't need him worming his way back into the soft parts of her heart. She *wanted* to be mad. It felt good to have something to hold onto, something to drive her to do more than she'd done with her life.

And she realized that her suppressed anger had been what had kept her sane all these years. It wasn't until Boone had started showing her what she'd been missing that she'd even known what kind of life she could have.

She scuffed her feet along the sidewalk in front of the city buildings, the sky gray and threatening above her. But she didn't want to go back to her hotel yet. The microscopic room choked her, much the same way Three Rivers had.

What do I do now? she prayed, even tipping her head back to look into the heavens. How can I face everyone at church again? And how do I get rid of these furious feelings toward Boone?

She felt the same way about him now as she had when he'd moved to town. Stolen her clinic. Strutted around the animal hospital like he'd founded the town, built the building, and single-handedly saved every animal in Texas.

Nicole hated this corner of herself. The one where her thoughts were venomous and built on untruths. She'd spent a year in that corner, Boone the one keeping her there.

Boone.

Even as she thought his name, she realized how horrible she was being. The anger in her gut started to dissipate, but she gripped it with an iron fist and kept it close, close, close.

Because then she could think. Then, things got done. Then, she didn't have to admit that she was weak and the one to blame for everything that had happened.

* * *

Nicole returned to her life in Three Rivers, just like she'd always known she would. Sure, she dreamt of a life in Amarillo, or Austin, or maybe even New Orleans. But she knew she'd never be able to leave Three Rivers as long as her parents were here.

By the time she got to the clinic, Boone had already taken his first patient back. Secretly, she was glad. She didn't want the first place she saw him to be the clinic, in front of Joanne and the other people who worked there.

She'd closed her office door, a real irregularity for her, but Joanne knocked on it at the same time she opened it. She re-shut it behind her and perched on the edge of the chair across from Nicole.

"How are you?"

"Just fine."

Joanne wrung her hands. "Are you sure?"

"Joanne," Nicole said in her best office administrator voice.

"Everyone feels so bad," she said anyway. "Pastor Scott has called me twice a day, asking about you. Says you won't answer your phone. Poor Brother Myron has baked himself enough cookies to raise hundreds of dollars at a bake sale. We're all just so worried."

Nicole's shoulders drooped as the fight left her body. She was tired of being so weak and pretending not to be. "I could use some cookies probably." She attempted to smile. "Did I ruin the entire Christmas program?"

"Of course not." Joanne reached across the desk and put both of her hands on Nicole's.

Nicole pulled her hands away. She didn't like being

touched when she was stressed. Boone knew that. Boone gave her space. At least he used to.

Joanne left, only to be replaced by Boone before ten minutes had passed. "Seriously?" she said when he poked his head through the door he'd just opened. "I'm not going to get any work done today."

"I just wanted to say hi."

"Hi." She folded her arms on her desk and drank him in. He seemed different. Or maybe that was her. The same simmering annoyance that she'd experienced with Boone when he'd first moved to Three Rivers bubbled in her bloodstream now.

But why? she asked herself. She didn't particularly want to go back to her dreary, overlooked existence. But it felt good to be mad at him for some reason.

He ducked out and closed the door, obviously able to feel her animosity though she hadn't said anything too terrible. She sighed. It didn't matter what she said. Boone had always been able to feel her mood.

He didn't come in again, and while she usually stayed late with him on Thursdays, tonight she left when Joanne did. She ran by her parents' and made sure they were okay, then she went home. She wandered through her backyard, her mind spinning through the events of the past few days.

Boone showed up about eight-thirty, a pizza box in one hand and a single red rose in the other. He didn't say anything as he sat beside her on the bench in the backyard.

She took the rose and he balanced the pizza box on his knees.

"I'm really sorry," he finally said.

"It's fine."

"I've dated a lot of women."

Her gaze flew to his and he looked at her like he was trying to really see inside her mind. She glanced away.

After he cleared his throat, he said, "I've dated a lot of women, and when one says something is fine, it's usually not."

"It really is." Nicole didn't want to explain herself. She leaned her head against Boone's shoulder and linked her hand through his elbow, trying to sort through her own feelings.

They felt tied up, jumbled, chained together in strange ways.

He relaxed next to her, something that lightened the mood. He stayed for an hour and then headed home. She padded into her kitchen, where she found Taz and Valcor curled up in the same kennel. "Why can't I accept his apology?" she whispered to the dark house and the snoozing dogs.

He'd brought food, flowers, all the right words. And still Nicole felt stitched together wrong. She told herself she just needed more time and everything would work itself out.

* * *

A WEEK PASSED. The New Year came. Everything between her and Boone stayed cool, almost like the sizzle that had existed there had fizzled out. He only kissed her once, and finally, he showed up at her house early on a Friday morning wearing those skimpy shorts and that tight, silky T-shirt.

"Can I come in?" he asked.

It wasn't exactly cold in Texas in January, but it wasn't warm either. She stepped back to allow him space to enter.

"This isn't working for me," he said maintaining eye contact. "I don't think it's working for you either."

Tears came immediately, but she nodded as she employed all her willpower to keep her eyes dry.

"I don't know what I did." His shoulders remained boxy, his voice strong, his eyes unyielding. Irritation sang through her. He could at least pretend like he felt bad about breaking up with her. "I've apologized a bunch of times. I don't know what else to do."

Nicole didn't either. She hadn't been able to move past her mental block with Boone, with Pastor Scott, with God.

Boone's jaw clenched, twitched, clamped, tensed. "So that's it?"

She didn't know what he wanted her to say.

"Are you going to say anything?" He folded his arms across his chest. Her heart cracked and bled. She wasn't sure why she was allowing this when she loved him.

Tell him! her heart screamed. Say something!

Pain and anger and absolute agony streamed across his

face. "I'll see you at work." He turned and wrenched open the door, leaving with long strides. "Come on, guys," he said to his dogs. The last thing she heard was the gentle slap of his sneakers as he ran away from her house.

Nicole let the tears fall then. She retreated to the only sanctuary she had left—the backyard, where she stayed for the rest of the day. She wasn't sure what exactly had happened over the past couple of weeks. Most of the time she felt detached from her body, going through the motions at work and home.

And now she'd lost Boone. Because of her love affair with her anger and her unwillingness to forgive, she'd lost Boone.

Chapter Twenty-Three

Boone poured himself into his marathon training. With only a month to go until the marathon, he couldn't afford to slack on his diet and exercise regimen. Which was just fine, because he didn't have anything else motivating him anymore.

He ignored Nicole at work as much as possible. A week after he'd stopped by her house and they'd broken up, he entered the clinic a few minutes late.

"There you are." Nicole stormed from her office, her anger like a scent on the wind.

"Here I am." He tried to edge to the right and get down the hall to his office, and fast, because her anger floated on the air the way the scent of maple syrup and butter did down by the pancake house.

"Your paperwork from last night is incomplete." She slapped it against his chest.

Joanne stood. "Nicole."

Nicole silenced her with a glare. Theo and Jack, who both helped with the animals in the clinic, entered the reception area. Theo stopped talking to Jack and they watched the scene before them.

"I'll finish it." Boone took the paperwork, unsure of what he'd missed. Whatever it was, he'd figure it out behind the closed door of his office. He turned and started toward the hall Theo and Jack were currently blocking.

"Do you need help reading it?" Nicole asked.

Time slowed as Boone turned, as Nicole said, "What with your dyslexia and all."

The knife of her words went straight into his heart, twisted, and got pulled out. He struggled for air as a blazing pain shot through his chest and into his head.

Joanne gasped and stared at Boone, and Theo and Jack scuffled their feet behind him.

He had no idea what he'd done to Nicole that was so horrible. All he knew was she was not the same person he'd fallen in love with. She wasn't even the same, awful person he'd encountered when he first moved here.

No, this version of the blonde-haired beauty he loved was vindictive and vicious. Way more than annoyance wound through him. Hurt. Humiliation. He glanced at Joanne and then back to Nicole.

"I can handle it," he said, ducking his head. He turned to find Theo's and Jack's eyes on him too, wide and wondering. He squeezed past them and went into his office, his already broken heart completely crushed.

He dialed Cash as soon as he locked the door behind him. "Hey, Doctor Drew," he started. "Is that job still available in Amarillo?" Boone twisted in his chair, sure it was time to move on. He couldn't stay here in Three Rivers and keep working with Nicole. The pain was too real, too immediate, never-ending.

Especially now that she'd been downright cruel to him. For the life of him, he couldn't figure out what he'd done to deserve such treatment. He wondered if her siblings had done something recently, if her mama had digressed further, or if her embarrassment over the Christmas program was really that upsetting to her.

If it was, she'd never forgive him for pushing her to sing in the choir, for coming up on the stand as if he could assist her.

Something she'd said about his father's questions over Thanksgiving popped into his mind. *He wanted to know if you'd interfered in my life yet.*

The air left Boone's lungs. He had. He *had* interfered in her life, and that was why she hated him now.

Definitely time to move on, he thought as Cash said, "I haven't found a partner yet."

"I'm already on my way," Boone said. He made arrangements to meet with Cash in a couple of weeks, just before the marathon, and hung up. He made it through the day without encountering Nicole again, even when he'd corrected his paperwork and stopped by her office to drop it off. He tossed it on her desk and made a hasty escape.

At home, he started a moving checklist, with items like "reserve a Dumpster" and "order boxes." He spent an hour on the Internet looking for somewhere to live in Amarillo. Through it all, a sense of discomfort threaded through him. He'd never felt like this before, like what he was doing wasn't right.

He'd left home with a bounce in his step and bright eyes for the future despite his father's warnings and his mother's sad countenance. He'd sacrificed sleep so he could study when his roommates wouldn't be able to see his struggle to read and been nothing but happy in college. He'd come to Three Rivers though the town was a bit too small for his tastes, his extended family a bit too close for comfort, and the possibilities endless and his opportunities wide open.

And he'd fallen in love with the town. Nicole. Riding horses out at Three Rivers. The ranch. His cousin and the community Squire had built.

The people of Three Rivers—and their pets. Even the pastor. He chuckled at the irony of it and let his thoughts linger on his family. They'd always been faithful, and though Boone had deviated from that for a short time, he'd enjoyed his return to church, to God.

What should I be doing? he pleaded. I can't stay here. But is Amarillo where I'm supposed to go?

He half-hoped the house would shake and a voice of

thunder would detail exactly what he should do. Of course it didn't. God often spoke in a quiet way. So quiet, Boone had to really be listening to hear Him.

He strained for the slightest whisper of direction as he accomplished a couple of items on his list and headed to bed. Lord Vader and Princess Leia jumped onto the bed with him, and he cradled one on each side.

"At least you guys still like me, right?"

Vader put his head in Boone's lap and peered up at him with doleful dog eyes. It seemed like he was asking where Nicole was, and a knot of emotion worked its way into Boone's throat.

He couldn't remember the last time he'd cried, but he felt like emptying all this turmoil inside him and crying seemed to be the best way to do that. But the tears didn't come. His agony went on and on, and the fact that Nicole had thrown his biggest weakness to the wolves drove fury through him with the force of gravity.

"We can't stay here," he said to the dogs. Neither of them answered, but Leia snuggled in closer and he stroked her head. "I think you guys will like it in Amarillo."

The real question was if Boone would like it in Amarillo—and if it was far enough away from Nicole to mend his broken heart.

* * *

He didn't have to tell Nicole he was leaving Puppy Pawz or Three Rivers, so he didn't. He could put the place up for sale without her expertise or knowledge.

Telling Squire about the move was the hardest, but he handled it well with a simple, "I'm sorry to hear that, Boone. What's next for you?"

A pang of homesickness hit Boone square in the chest. He took an extra moment to compose himself before he said, "I'm looking to go to Amarillo for a while."

"Amarillo's a nice place," he said.

"Sure is." Boone smiled, the urge to call his mother growing stronger by the moment. His mother had grown up in Amarillo, and both of his grandparents had lived there for years and years. They'd run the seed and feed shop where his parents had met, and one of her sisters still managed the place.

"Well, I suppose we'll just need a forwarding address. You can leave it with Garth. He'll get you your last paycheck." Squire looked at him, his eyes narrowed. "You sure you can't make the drive a couple times a week? You can just stay on."

"I don't know what it'll be like in Amarillo," Boone said. "I'm meeting with him when I go for the marathon."

"Well, the door's always open," Squire said.

"Thank you," Boone said. "I've sure enjoyed my time here in Three Rivers." His voice broke on the last word and he finished the conversation quickly. Back in the safety of his truck, he ran his hands over his beard and up to his head. He felt lost. Nothing more. Nothing less.

A stranger in a strange land, he thought, wondering how he'd gone from knowing exactly what he wanted—to spend the rest of his days with Nicole in Three Rivers—to feeling like someone had scooped him out with a melon baller.

* * *

ON HIS LAST day at Puppy Pawz, he waited until Nicole went to lunch before gathering everyone into the lobby. He handed Joanne a piece of paper with his new address in Amarillo on it and turned to the people he'd worked with for almost twenty months.

He grinned at them while Joanne brought out the cupcakes he'd picked up at the bakery that morning. "It's my last day though the place hasn't sold yet," he said. "It will. I know it will. There's already an offer that's supposed to be coming in."

Boone just hadn't been able to accept Louis Whitby's offer quite yet, though it was fair. He'd been toying with the idea of keeping Puppy Pawz and just employing Louis as the vet. But that would require a lot of conversation with Nicole, and well, she and Boone weren't exactly on speaking terms.

He cleared his throat, wishing his thoughts were as easily organized. "And I wanted to say goodbye." He went around to each person and handed them a note he'd written for them. "I've enjoyed working with each of you."

It felt wrong that he hadn't told Nicole about this goodbye party, that he'd deliberately waited until she was out of the office to hand out treats and cards.

"I wrote these myself," he said. "No computer. So if you have trouble reading them, I apologize." He looked at Joanne and put a smile on his face that wasn't as hard as he thought it would be. "Sometimes my dyslexia isn't kind when I'm writing."

"Boone," Joanne said, tears brimming in her eyes. "We'll miss you." She clutched him in a tight hug. "No one cares about the dyslexia."

"Nicole does," he whispered, stepping back and meeting Joanne's gaze.

A tear fell and she swiped at it. "She'll come around. She just needs—"

"Please don't tell her where I went," he said, nodding to that piece of paper she'd laid casually on her desk. "If I wanted her to know, I'd tell her."

Joanne sniffed and nodded, tucking the paper under a notebook and turning to wipe her eyes.

Boone enjoyed half a cupcake with his co-workers and friends and then took a couple of boxes from his office to his car. He turned back to Puppy Pawz and gave it one final look before ducking into his car and driving away.

Chapter Twenty-Four

Nicole arrived at her parents' house by nine o'clock on Saturday morning, beyond relieved it was the weekend. And Boone spent Monday at the ranch, so Nicole had the next seventy-two hours where she could at least breathe without wondering if he'd walk in and confront her.

Pure guilt pulled her stomach tight as she walked through the front door. She leaned in the doorway for support, still shocked at her behavior. She honestly couldn't remember outing Boone's dyslexia to the staff at Puppy Pawz, but Joanne insisted she had.

The next time she'd looked at Boone, she'd seen the raw pain in his eyes, the horrible hurt, and Nicole knew she'd done what Joanne had said she had. She needed to apologize, but she didn't know how. He wouldn't forgive her anyway. Some things were unforgivable.

If she could get out to Three Rivers Ranch and Courage Reins, she and Doughnut could work out a conversation she could have with Boone that included an apology. Maybe even a declaration of her love for him.

But she knew she'd never go out there by herself. That would almost be as painful as the past few weeks had been.

Mama slept in the recliner, and Nicole tried to rouse her. Mama didn't move. Concern spiked through her and she nudged her mother's shoulder. Nothing.

"Daddy?" she called, but he didn't come from the kitchen.

Fear Nicole had only felt one other time in her life—after she'd discovered that she'd humiliated Boone in the clinic—ran through her body like someone had replaced her blood with ice water. She left her non-responsive mother's side and checked the kitchen.

Empty. Daddy wasn't in the house or the backyard, but Nicole hadn't noticed that the car wasn't in the driveway. She looked now, and sure enough, her father's twenty-year-old car with the wood paneling was gone.

Nicole didn't know what to do next. Daddy never left Mama home alone. Maybe he'd panicked when he couldn't rouse her.

"Why don't you have a cell phone?" she asked, her voice so high-pitched she wondered if she was even herself anymore. She didn't feel like herself. She hadn't since the Christmas program.

And she didn't like who she'd become in the months since. She glanced up into the stormy sky. "What do I do now?"

No one answered. The neighborhood stayed as peaceful and quiet as it had always been. Nicole raged inside, her nerves teeming and tears streaming down her cheeks.

All at once, she calmed. The sun broke through the clouds for a few seconds, and Nicole knew what to do.

Mama first. Boone second.

She had some damage to undo and she could only hope that it wasn't irreparable.

Straightening her shoulders and wiping her face, she returned to the house, where she dialed 911.

She paced in her parents' living room, her mind racing through the serenity of the neighborhood. Then the ambulance arrived, and the paramedics began asking questions, and Daddy showed up with a bag of bagels from the bakery.

He went in the ambulance with Mama, and Nicole sat behind the wheel of her car, the road between Three Rivers and Amarillo miles and miles longer than it usually was. She parked near the emergency entrance, but she couldn't get herself to go inside. The sedan provided safety, and Nicole couldn't break the seal and pop that bubble.

Not without Boone, who had driven her to this hospital last time she'd been here.

A sense of hopelessness nearly drowned her, a feeling she hadn't experienced in a while. Since giving up her dreams and staying in Three Rivers. At least she didn't start crying again. She'd spent so much time crying lately, and she wanted to be stronger than that.

She wanted to be better than she was.

A better singer.

A better office administrator.

A better girlfriend.

A better human being.

She opened the door and started with one step at a time toward the emergency entrance.

One step, she told herself. One more. And then another.

MAMA STAYED IN THE HOSPITAL, unresponsive but alive. She'd fallen into a coma, and the doctors weren't sure why. Daddy wouldn't leave her side, but Nicole found she couldn't just sit in that tiny room, with those beige walls, the humming machines, the nurses coming in and out with no new results.

She left Sunday night and returned to her house, where she spent a long time in the shower, trying to get the stench of the hospital out of her hair. After all, she couldn't wait until Tuesday to see Boone—and she certainly didn't want her desperate and heartfelt apology to happen at Puppy Pawz, even behind his closed office door.

The very idea of going to his house and pouring out her heart to him, begging him to forgive her, made a fearsome tremor shake her entire body. She towel dried her hair, piled it on her head, and slipped into a pair of yoga pants and her favorite oversized sweatshirt.

The neighbors had taken Taz and Valcor, and she left them there, rationalizing that another hour wouldn't matter. She drove slowly, the blocks passing quickly, which made no sense.

She knew as soon as she pulled up to Boone's that he wasn't home. All his windows sat in darkness, but she pulled into his driveway anyway. She got out of the car and stepped down the front walk.

That was when she saw the For Sale sign staked in the front yard.

She froze, everything in her going numb. Was he gone already? How could he be gone and she not know?

Please don't let him be gone, she begged as she pulled out her phone.

Chapter Twenty-Five

Boone's phone rang, and the sight of Nicole's face on the screen simultaneously sent his heart to the top of his skull and to the bottom of his feet.

He ignored the call. When she called again, he determined to leave his phone in his apartment as he went for his second run of the day. He normally wouldn't do that, especially in a new city and on a ten-mile-run.

And he couldn't this time either. He silenced the phone and stuck it in the pocket of his hydration backpack. *Responsibility first*, he thought.

"Come on, guys," he said to the dogs, and they trotted to him from the giant window that overlooked the park. He put on their harnesses and leashed them before entering the hallway. He didn't want to upset the elderly lady down the hall, and though he'd only lived in this apartment for two days, he knew if he let Vader even take one step into the hallway while he wasn't on the leash that Mrs. Dennis would tattle to the HOA board.

Princess Leia wouldn't ride the elevator, so Boone took them down the stairs and started his circuit around the park. He couldn't find his rhythm, his thoughts circulating around the two phone calls.

What could she possibly want from him? She hadn't spoken to him—truly *spoken* to him—in a long time. Before they broke up even. He thought of the wedding in her backyard, the twinkling tea lights and how they'd lit her eyes with a glow so sexy Boone hadn't been able to draw a full breath.

He thought of her reassurances on the way home from Thanksgiving in Grape Seed Falls. The way her whole face had lit up at the dam and then the lake in Hill Country.

He thought about how much he'd told her, and what she'd shared with him. The love he had for her was still there, still choking him, still alive.

He stopped halfway through his run, unable to regulate his breathing and get in the right zone. Frustration rose to the back of his throat, coating it with bitterness. The marathon was in six days. He couldn't afford to abandon his training schedule because of a phone call.

And yet, he did. Nicole had called four times by the time he checked his phone, and he sank onto a bench in the park and took a deep breath before dialing her back.

She answered on the first ring with, "You moved?" She

didn't sound angry, but her voice was definitely in the squeaky range.

His stomach twisted. "Last time I checked, I didn't have to run anything past you before doing it."

"Where are you?"

"It's almost the marathon."

"So you're in Amarillo."

"Yes, Nicole, I'm in Amarillo." A flash of her tossing his dyslexia in his face scurried through his mind. "You had to call four times to confirm that? I've been telling you about the marathon for eight straight months." His anger bubbled and all the things he'd wanted to say—all the horrible, hurtful things he'd wanted to say—surged to the tip of his tongue. "You know, it wasn't my fault what happened at the Christmas program. You rehearsed the songs for weeks and weeks. You're a beautiful singer, and maybe I should've stayed in my seat, but I didn't. I can't change that I didn't, but it still wasn't my fault you couldn't sing."

A pause made his skin crawl, and combined with Leia pulling on her leash, Boone got to his feet. "I don't have time for this, Nicole. We broke up—an event where you didn't say a single word. I don't owe you any more explanations."

He hung up before she could say anything. Boone glanced around the park, but no one seemed as unhappy as he was. Couples strolled hand in hand, and no one glanced his way. He felt invisible, alone, with this pain in his chest where his heart should be.

He swiped on his phone and made another call, but this time when the woman picked up, she said, "Boone, my sweet son, how are you?"

A smile stole across his face. "Hey, Mom. How's everyone?"

She trilled out a laugh. "Everyone's fine. The marathon is this weekend, right?"

She knew. Boone barely spoke with his parents and yet his mother knew about the marathon. He walked slowly toward the apartment building, his dogs coming along with him obediently.

"This weekend," he confirmed.

"And we'll be able to see the finish line online?"

"That's right, Mom." Fondness filled him, and he wondered if he really belonged in Amarillo. He glanced up into the sky, trying to listen to his emotions, his gut feelings, and God.

And he knew: He didn't belong in Amarillo.

Problem was, he didn't know where he belonged.

THE WEEK PASSED and Boone devoted every moment to his training, his marathon diet, and his dogs. He wasn't starting at the new animal hospital for another week, and he'd considered returning to his family's ranch for a visit.

Just to see how he felt when he went home, find out if he was supposed to be there instead of here.

Nicole hadn't called again, thankfully. Boone didn't want to let the negative, hurtful words out. They wouldn't help her, and they certainly wouldn't help him either.

He started the marathon, his feet finding the rhythm easily, his lungs working properly. It was a good day to run, so Boone ran.

The hours passed—three of them—and Boone hoped to reach the finish line before the fourth expired. He checked his watch at mile twenty-four. He was going to make it under four hours, and a sense of pride inflated his chest.

His feet kept moving. His breath whooshed in and out. Eventually the finish line approached, and a pang of regret that he didn't have anyone there cheering for him specifically stung for just a moment.

Then he crested the hill and saw the crowd about a half a mile up ahead. Pride swelled in his chest. He'd just run his first marathon!

A roar of noise met his ears, growing louder and louder until it was a cacophony of voices, all shouting and congratulating.

Somehow, through all that, he heard his name, which was unique enough that he knew it belonged to him.

"Boone! Go, Boone!"

He kept running, even as the voice separated itself from the myriad of other voices in the fray.

The voice belonged to Nicole.

He crossed the finish line, a huge smile on his face for his mother. He lifted his arms in victory and let his legs carry him several extra steps until he finally stopped. Pure euphoria filled him, and he turned to see if Nicole had really come.

He'd never specifically invited her to come watch him run, though he'd certainly talked about the marathon enough for her to know it was important to him.

Another runner stepped out of the way, and she appeared, her face just as beautiful as ever. She wore a distinctly hopeful look and approached like she wasn't sure if he'd attack her or embrace her.

His heart skipped a beat, and then two. He was still in love with her, despite what she'd said and what she'd done.

"You just *ran a marathon*," she said, a smile forming on her face. "It was incredible."

He wasn't sure if it was the adrenaline from all the endorphins, but a smile popped onto his face too. "I just ran a marathon."

She gestured behind her, where a giant screen listed the runners and their final scores. "Not only that, but you finished in the men's top ten."

His attention shot to the scoreboard screen. The list cycled through and he waited to see his name. When it finally came up, it was listed as number nine.

Surprise kept his pulse bouncing in his neck, and pure joy made him turn toward Nicole and sweep her off her feet, a laugh flying into the sky. He forgot that they weren't together. He forgot that she wasn't his to kiss. He forgot the pain he'd endured since Christmas.

She laughed too and when he set her on her feet, the chaos around them melted into silence, into nothing. "Why did you come?" He kept his hands on her waist, kept her close.

"This was important to you."

"Why did you tell everyone about my dyslexia?"

Her eyes turned scared and she shook her head. "I honestly don't know. I got...lost. I blamed you for what happened at the program, because it was easier than blaming myself."

"Blamed? Past tense?" Boone wasn't sure why it mattered. She needed to do a lot more than come cheer him at the finish line to make up for what she'd done.

No she doesn't, he thought. He knew Nicole Hymas, and she didn't do anything she didn't want to. She didn't leave Three Rivers easily.

"I don't blame you anymore," she said. "I'm still working on myself." She drew in a deep breath. "I am a horrible, horrible person. I know this, Boone." She gazed up at him, her green eyes so intense. "I am so, so sorry. I cannot apologize enough."

His heart softened. "I know you are, sweetheart." He reached up and brushed her hair off her face. "But that still might not be enough. I have a new job here."

"I'm in love with you," she said, her voice strong and

her eyes warm and wonderful. "And you haven't sold the animal hospital, despite Louis Whitby having an offer in on it for weeks."

Boone still loved her too, and his heart felt caught between two impossible situations. He sighed. "Sometimes love isn't enough."

"I refuse to believe that." She clung to his arms. "I don't think you believe that either."

He didn't, not really. But if there was one thing he knew, it was that once things happened, there was no going back. "Everything is different now."

"You're right. You're different. I'm different."

Boone stared down at her, realizing that his Nicole had returned. She wasn't the vindictive, vicious woman who'd shouted his secret to the entire clinic.

"I'm sorry," she whispered. "I will say it over and over, because I mean it. If I could go back in time." She cleared her throat. "I would. I would go back in time and fix that. Fix myself before I met you so I wasn't so screwed up. Fix things with my siblings so I didn't blame you for every little thing that goes wrong." She sighed and paced away from him. "I know it's not your fault I couldn't sing at the Christmas program."

When she looked back at him, raw fear rode in her expression. "It was mine. Everything that's happened since then has been *my* fault."

Boone had never felt the cleansing power of forgiveness as acutely as he did then. "It doesn't matter," he said.

"It's done. Over." He opened his arms to her and she came to him, a wobbly smile on her face.

"I love you," he whispered into her hair. He wasn't sure where he should be living or what he should be doing, but he knew that.

"Mama's really sick," she said. "Daddy won't leave her side."

He held her at arm's length. "Nicole?" Tears trickled down her cheeks and he tenderly wiped them away. "Talk to me."

"I don't want—I mean, I want someone by my side when I can't remember who I am, holding my hand and telling me stories of how we fell in love." She inhaled deeply and let it out slowly. "I want *you* to be that man, Boone."

"And I want to be that man," he whispered just before he leaned down and pressed a kiss to her lips.

Chapter Twenty-Six

Nicole woke the next morning with a song in her head. She stayed in bed as the lyrics to *Respect* by Aretha Franklin flowed through her head. She smiled and pulled the covers to her chin.

Her songs were back.

She was back.

She'd stayed up late last night, beyond grateful for the easy way Boone had forgiven her. She hadn't quite been able to do that, and she'd stayed on her knees for a long time, trying to figure out if she deserved his forgiveness.

She'd been so cruel. So stubborn. So out of her mind.

She still didn't feel one-hundred-percent like herself, but Boone's last words had helped. *I loved you once, Nicole. I know the woman I fell for is in there somewhere.*

Nicole hoped she was. She'd prayed for it last night. Dreamt about a future with Boone. They hadn't talked much more about heavy things. He'd taken her for a late lunch and told her about the animal hospital here in Amarillo. Because she feared the answer, she hadn't asked him if he was going to stay.

But she didn't want him to stay. So she stretched and reached for her phone, typing out a quick *Breakfast?* and sending it to him.

In Three Rivers, she'd already be showered and ready for church, only moments away from walking out the door to get to her parents' house. She fought the urge to call Daddy at the hospital. She'd be going home today, and she'd stop by and see them both before she left Amarillo.

Her phone chimed several times, one sound almost on top of another. She glanced at it, and saw messages from Boone, as well as Gary, her oldest brother and Elaine, her sister.

She went to Boone's first, because she knew it would put a smile on her face. *Sure. I'll come get you in a half hour.*

She confirmed just as a message from Jordan came in. Her siblings had all gotten her message, obviously, and she wondered if they'd collaborated before they'd returned her text.

Gary's said: What do you mean, Mama's dying?
Elaine's: I can help make the funeral arrangements.
Jordan's: Is it really that bad?
No thanks for letting us know, Nicole.

You're so great, staying there and taking care of every-thing, Nicole.

We love you, Nicole.

She sighed, only allowing the hateful, negative thoughts to linger for a few heartbeats. Her siblings were who they were. It didn't matter if Nicole craved a closer relationship with them. It wasn't going to happen—something she'd realized while sitting in the hospital room with Mama.

It didn't matter what Nicole wanted. She could pray and pray and cry and cry, and Mama still wasn't going to get better.

She released her animosity toward her siblings and answered their texts. *I mean Mama's in a coma and she's not going to wake up.*

I would love your help with funeral arrangements.

It's really that bad. Clear some time in your schedule to come back to Three Rivers for the funeral. Soon.

Then she braided her hair and changed out of her pajamas. She silenced her phone so she wouldn't have to do any more family business during her breakfast date with Boone. After all, she still had a long way to go to make things right with him.

She arrived in the lobby just as he pulled into the circle drive. Increasing her step, she practically skipped out to meet him.

"Hey." He got out of his truck, leaned against it, and

grinned at her. It was the sexiest thing she'd ever seen, and she lifted up on her toes and kissed him.

He chuckled against her mouth before properly kissing her. "So it's a *good* morning," he said.

"I woke up with a song in my head," she said.

Confusion blipped through his expression. "Doesn't that happen everyday?"

She shook her head and traced her fingers up the side of his face to his head. "It stopped for a while."

He blinked at her and asked, "What's the song for today?"

"Respect."

"Ah, the oldies. I like that." He lifted one of her braids and looked at it. "I'm sorry you lost your songs for a while. I know how much you love them."

A thought entered her mind and burst from her throat. "I think I'm going to ask Pastor Scott if I can sing at Easter."

Boone simply looked at her, his gaze even and his jaw tight. He finally said, "I'll stay home that day."

"You don't think it's a good idea?"

"The last time didn't go so well, and I'm not interested in repeating it."

A white hot knife of regret lanced through her. She'd really hurt him, even more than she knew. "I'm sorry," she said, her lips barely moving with the words.

"I'm starving," he said, looking away and changing the subject quite rapidly. "Where should we eat?"

"I don't know. I've only spent a day or two in Amarillo outside the hospital," she said, and he paused in turning to open the door.

"How do waffles sound?"

A smile swept across her face. "Waffles sound great. Do they have Belgian waffles?"

"I'm sure they do. A Belgian waffle you shall have." He opened her door for her, and Nicole climbed onto the bench seat, grateful for another chance with Boone.

* * *

SIX MONTHS LATER:

"I've got the lights." Boone grabbed the box from the storage shed and dropped a kiss on Nicole's forehead as he went into the yard. Warmth covered her from head to toe, the only cool spot where Princess Leia licked her shoulder.

She laughed and pushed the dog away. "Go chase Valcor," she said. "I'm working." She continued to dig through the boxes on the lowest shelf, searching for the garden gnomes Mama had loved. She finally found them and pulled the box toward her, feeling the gritty dust under her fingers.

As always, a pang of sadness accompanied the thought of Mama. She'd passed away before Easter, before Nicole had an opportunity to show her mother how brave she was —and how gifted.

Since that successful performance, Nicole had been

singing in the church choir regularly, and never once had that paralyzing fear returned.

Boone had, though. He'd packed up and come back to Three Rivers without ever starting at the animal hospital in Amarillo. She'd asked him once if he regretted that decision, and he'd said, "I knew I wasn't supposed to be in Amarillo." He'd glanced around the dog park where they'd stood. "Three Rivers is home now."

He'd tucked her into his side, made room for her in his life, kissed her like a man in love.

"Hey." He poked his head back into the shed. "The bride just called and wants to know if she can have the bridge."

Nicole heaved herself to her feet. "I'll call her back."

He filled the doorway and wouldn't move. "I want to ask you something first."

She dusted her hands off on her shorts. "All right." She tucked an errant piece of hair behind her ear, feeling dirty from top to bottom.

He reached for her hand and drew her out of the shed and into the yard. She let him take her over to the orchard, where he'd hung the fairy lights for the wedding taking place there the following evening.

"Nicole." He paused beneath an apricot tree. "I love you. I said I wanted to be the man who would be at your side when you couldn't remember who you were. I want to tell you the story of how we fell in love." He dropped to one knee, and Nicole's heart did back handsprings through her chest.

"Boone," she whispered, her hands going to her throat.

"Will you marry me?" He produced a ring box seemingly out of thin air and cracked the lid.

She didn't look at the ring. Couldn't look away from Boone's beautiful dark eyes, so filled with love, hope, adoration, and more hope.

"Yes," she said, laughter following. He rose to his feet and she launched herself into his arms. "Yes."

He laughed with her and kissed her. Again, this kiss felt totally new, existing on a completely different sphere than any they'd shared before. Because now she was kissing her fiancé.

Keep reading for a sneak peek of the next book in the Three Rivers Ranch Romance™ series, **The Sleigh on Seventeenth Street**.

Sneak Peek! The Sleigh on Seventeenth Street

Dylan Walker parked his truck and peered through the windshield at the mobile trailer that had been set up. Beyond that sat the Texas wilderness with trees, wild grasses, and beautiful flowers. A sour sensation coated his stomach. He couldn't believe the City Council had approved this development. Hundred-year-old trees would be lost. More of Three Rivers to enjoy, sure, but less of nature. And that didn't sit right in Dylan's gut.

Once he got out of the truck and made it a few steps, the highway that led out to Three Rivers Ranch glistened in the morning light. It had rained earlier, and the scent of dust and water mingled in the air.

Dylan took a deep breath and said a silent prayer. *Please let us get this bid.* He'd been working on the electrician bid for this new housing development for a solid month. The city desperately needed the contract, and he wanted to be the one to bring it to them.

With the project taking over two years, with four stages as new homes, twin homes, and condos went in, Dylan wanted to be in every residence, wiring every light and every surround sound system.

He shouldn't care so much. He'd get paid no matter what. But he and his boss had developed a plan to increase the public perception of the Three Rivers Electric Company, and if they won this bid, it would go a long way in proving to the citizens that the Electric Company was dedicated to providing excellent electrical customer service to all residents.

Dylan squared his shoulders, climbed the steps to the door, and entered the trailer. How the door had kept so much chaos concealed was a mystery. Dylan's head swiveled left and right as he took in the mob before him.

He recognized a dark-haired man, who'd come from Amarillo to bid on the electrical work for the build. Dylan had seen him—and lost a bid to him—at an office building last year. His mood darkened when he caught sight of yet another competitor, this one approaching him.

"Hiya, Dylan," the man said. Darrel maybe? Dallin?

"Hey," Dylan said, going with a more masculine greeting and bypassing the man's name completely. It wasn't like they were friends.

"You got your bid?" Darrel-or-Dallin nodded toward the folder Dylan held.

He clutched it tighter, a blip of annoyance coasting through him. "Yeah." Everyone here had a bid. Saddleback Homes had announced six weeks ago that they'd be taking bids for one day only. Eight hours. They'd look at all of them by the following day, when all the contractors, plumbers, electricians, and tradesmen had to be present in order to accept the bid.

Dylan had never seen anything like their process. He supposed it would make things go faster, and he'd cleared his schedule for tomorrow, his hopes high.

He'd arrived at the build site fifteen minutes early, thinking he might be the only one in the trailer for a few minutes, hoping to have a chance to speak with the manager of the project for a moment.

That wasn't going to happen. Dylan moved away from the door when someone opened it behind him. Thankfully, the other electrician got lost in the crowd. Dylan glanced around, his claustrophobic tendencies rearing themselves against the back of his throat. His pulse accelerated, and the sea of people and noise and activity before him started to blend into one giant wall of color.

He made a beeline for the door, glad for the cooler air outside of that room. It couldn't be bigger than a railcar, yet it held at least two dozen people. Dylan leaned against the railing and sucked in lungful after lungful of oxygen.

"Dylan Walker," a woman said, and he blinked.

His blurred vision took several moments to refocus, and when it did, he soaked in the form of Camila Cruz standing on the second step from the top. Golden-brown eyes he could swim in if she'd let him. Waves of nearly black, wavy hair. Yards of dark skin. *Fiery Latina temper*, he reminded himself as she did not look pleased to see him, which somehow made her more attractive.

"Cami." Dylan had entertained thoughts of dating Camila a few years ago, but she had one massive chip on her shoulder during a project they'd completed together. She was headstrong, and stubborn, and bossy. Beautiful, absolutely. And Dylan didn't mind a strong, take-charge kind of woman. But Camila put off a vibe that said she definitely wasn't interested in him, so he'd kept his thoughts to himself.

Cami worked for the only plumber in town, a mom and pop joint that relied on the residents of Three Rivers to stay afloat. A winning bid for a project this size would allow Abraham and Dana Sheraton to retire. Maybe that was why Cami looked like she'd swallowed poison and was about to throw up.

"Why are you out here?" she asked.

"Lots of people in there," he said, adding a shrug to the sentence so it would seem more casual. "I figure I have eight hours to put in my bid. I don't need to stand in line or practice my pitch."

She nodded and finished climbing the steps. Though she wore a gray T-shirt and jeans, Dylan still noticed her curves as she passed him and opened the door. The noise coming from inside nearly convinced him to leave and come back later, but he couldn't return to the office without turning in the bid. His boss would fillet him with a single look.

So he followed Cami into the trailer, noticing how rigid she stood. "Told ya," he said.

"There are at least four other plumbers here," she said, her gaze swinging around the way his had.

"It's a big project."

"As if I didn't know." She rolled her eyes and hipped her way through the crowd to the far end of the trailer, where a table had been set up. Dylan watched her, almost intoxicated by the leftover whiff of perfume she'd left behind and the capable way she found what she was looking for.

He finally tore his gaze from her when she glanced over her shoulder to where he stood, as if she could somehow feel him watching her. He took a deep breath and looked around the trailer. He realized that hardly anyone held a folder the way he did. They were mingling and talking and looking at huge posters that had been put on the walls, detailing the phases of the build.

He moved through the press of bodies until he got to the end of the trailer too. A single man stood behind the table, which bore trays labeled *Plumbing, Electricity, Floors, Painting, General Contractors,* and several more titles.

He put his folder in the appropriate tray, ready to leave. These other men—and Cami—might not have anything to do for the rest of the day, but Dylan did. He turned to go, nearly mowing Cami to the ground in the process. Why was she standing so close?

"Sorry," he mumbled, sidestepping her and getting out of that trailer.

* * *

THAT EVENING FOUND him at home, without Boone's pets to take care of. Without anything to eat, as his mom hardly cooked at all anymore. But when she did, Dylan ate like a king for days. Boone too. And Boone's dogs.

Dylan could put together scrambled eggs and toast, so he did that. He sometimes went over to his best friend's house to watch a baseball game, but there wasn't a game he cared about tonight. And now that Boone and Nicole were dating, Dylan wasn't always welcome in the evenings.

With summer in full swing and the holidays on the horizon, Dylan only had loneliness to look forward to. He'd attend Labor Day barbeques, Halloween parties, and Thanksgiving dinner at his parent's house on the other side of town with all three of his sisters, their husbands, and all of their kids.

Two of them still lived here in Three Rivers, and the other lived in Parma, only a half an hour away. Every Sunday was like Thanksgiving, and the thought of attending another family get-together by himself—even if he did love playing with his nieces and nephews—made him grumpy.

The TV blared in front of him, but he wasn't paying attention to it. He mentally ran through the female prospects in his life. He needed someone to take to the next family event, if only so he wouldn't have to go alone.

He'd dated several women in town, and since he'd grown up right here in Three Rivers, some girls were off the table. He may have dated them in high school, or they knew too much about him, or he them.

Round and round he went, and the only name he could come up with was Camila.

"Don't be ridiculous," he muttered to himself as he took his empty plate into the kitchen. He left it in the sink, along with the rest of his dishes from that week. He'd get to them on Sunday morning, the way he always did.

"Cami will chew you up and spit you out." Dylan stood in his kitchen, the rest of the house silent, empty, sad. Maybe he needed someone to challenge him. Maybe —he scoffed and returned to the couch. He wanted the Saddleback project, and he wanted someone to talk to at night. Didn't mean that person was Camila Cruz, and he found himself hoping that she didn't win the plumbing bid.

Guilt threaded through him, but he managed to calm it enough to fall asleep. His dreams featured a honey-eyed woman, whose waves of dark hair flew behind her as she walked toward him. She wore a plumbing tool belt, and she was still the most beautiful thing Dream-Dylan had ever seen.

* * *

Find out if Dylan and Cami can make water and electricity mix this Christmas season! **Look for THE SLEIGH ON SEVENTEENTH STREET by scanning the QR code below!**

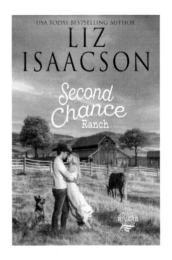

Second Chance Ranch: A Three Rivers Ranch Romance™ (Book 1): After his deployment, injured and discharged Major Squire Ackerman returns to Three Rivers Ranch, wanting to forgive Kelly for ignoring him a decade ago. He'd like to provide the stable life she needs, but with old wounds opening and a ranch on the brink of financial collapse, it will take patience and faith to make their second chance possible.

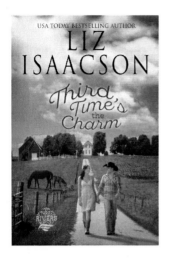

Third Time's the Charm: A Three Rivers Ranch Romance™ (Book 2): First Lieutenant Peter Marshall has a truckload of debt and no way to provide for a family, but Chelsea helps him see past all the obstacles, all the scars. With so many unknowns, can Pete and Chelsea develop the love, acceptance, and faith needed to find their happily ever after?

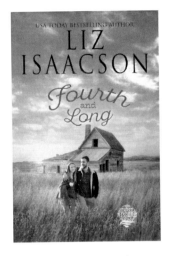

Fourth and Long: A Three Rivers Ranch Romance™ (Book 3): Commander Brett Murphy goes to Three Rivers Ranch to find some rest and relaxation with his Army buddies. Having his ex-wife show up with a seven-year-old she claims is his son is anything but the R&R he craves. Kate needs to make amends, and Brett needs to find forgiveness, but are they too late to find their happily ever after?

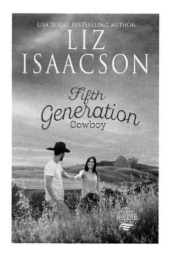

Fifth Generation Cowboy: A Three Rivers Ranch Romance™ (Book 4): Tom Lovell has watched his friends find their true happiness on Three Rivers Ranch, but everywhere he looks, he only sees friends. Rose Reyes has been bringing her daughter out to the ranch for equine therapy for months, but it doesn't seem to be working. Her challenges with Mari are just as frustrating as ever. Could Tom be exactly what Rose needs? Can he remove his friendship blinders and find love with someone who's been right in front of him all this time?

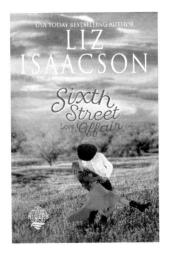

Sixth Street Love Affair: A Three Rivers Ranch Romance™ (Book 5): After losing his wife a few years back, Garth Ahlstrom thinks he's ready for a second chance at love. But Juliette Thompson has a secret that could destroy their budding relationship. Can they find the strength, patience, and faith to make things work?

The Seventh Sergeant: A Three Rivers Ranch Romance™ (Book 6): Life has finally started to settle down for Sergeant Reese Sanders after his devastating injury overseas. Discharged from the Army and now with a good job at Courage Reins, he's finally found happiness—until a horrific fall puts him right back where he was years ago: Injured and depressed. Carly Watters, Reese's new veteran care coordinator, dislikes small towns almost as much as she loathes cowboys. But she finds herself faced with both when she gets assigned to Reese's case. Do they have the humility and faith to make their relationship more than professional?

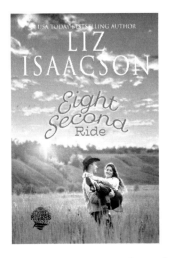

Eight Second Ride: A Three Rivers Ranch Romance™ (Book 7): Ethan Greene loves his work at Three Rivers Ranch, but he can't seem to find the right woman to settle down with. When sassy yet vulnerable Brynn Bowman shows up at the ranch to recruit him back to the rodeo circuit, he takes a different approach with the barrel racing champion. His patience and newfound faith pay off when a friendship--and more--starts with Brynn. But she wants out of the rodeo circuit right when Ethan wants to rejoin. Can they find the path God wants them to take and still stay together?

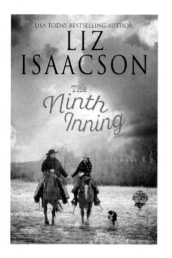

The Ninth Inning: A Three Rivers Ranch Romance™ (Book 8): The Christmas season has never felt like such a burden to boutique owner Andrea Larsen. But with Mama gone and the holidays upon her, Andy finds herself wishing she hadn't been so quick to judge her former boyfriend, cowboy Lawrence Collins. Well, Lawrence hasn't forgotten about Andy either, and he devises a plan to get her out to the ranch so they can reconnect. Do they have the faith and humility to patch things up and start a new relationship?

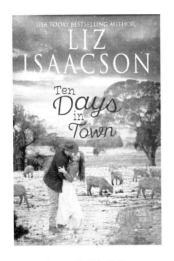

Ten Days in Town: A Three Rivers Ranch Romance™ (Book 9): Sandy Keller is tired of the dating scene in Three Rivers. Though she owns the pancake house, she's looking for a fresh start, which means an escape from the town where she grew up. When her older brother's best friend, Tad Jorgensen, comes to town for the holidays, it is a balm to his weary soul. A helicopter tour guide who experienced a near-death experience, he's looking to start over too--but in Three Rivers. Can Sandy and Tad navigate their troubles to find the path God wants them to take--and discover true love--in only ten days?

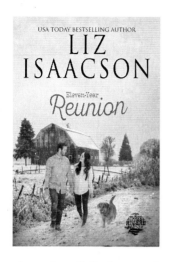

Eleven Year Reunion: A Three Rivers Ranch Romance™ (Book 10): Pastry chef extraordinaire, Grace Lewis has moved to Three Rivers to help Heidi Ackerman open a bakery in Three Rivers. Grace relishes the idea of starting over in a town where no one knows about her failed cupcakery. She doesn't expect to run into her old high school boyfriend, Jonathan Carver. A carpenter working at Three Rivers Ranch, Jon's in town against his will. But with Grace now on the scene, Jon's thinking life in Three Rivers is suddenly looking up. But with her focus on baking and his disdain for small towns, can they make their eleven year reunion stick?

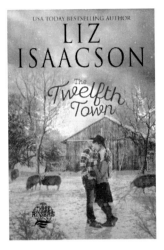

The Twelfth Town: A Three Rivers Ranch Romance™ (Book 11): Newscaster Taryn Tucker has had enough of life on-screen. She's bounced from town to town before arriving in Three Rivers, completely alone and completely anonymous--just the way she now likes it. She takes a job cleaning at Three Rivers Ranch, hoping for a chance to figure out who she is and where God wants her. When she meets happy-go-lucky cowhand Kenny Stockton, she doesn't expect sparks to fly. Kenny's always been "the best friend" for his female friends, but the pull between him and Taryn can't be denied. Will they have the courage and faith necessary to make their opposite worlds mesh?

Lucky Number Thirteen: A Three Rivers Ranch Romance™ (Book 12): Tanner Wolf, a rodeo champion ten times over, is excited to be riding in Three Rivers for the first time since he left his philandering ways and found religion. Seeing his old friends Ethan and Brynn is therapuetic--until a terrible accident lands him in the hospital. With his rodeo career over, Tanner thinks maybe he'll stay in town--and it's not just because his nurse, Summer Hamblin, is the prettiest woman he's ever met. But Summer's the queen of first dates, and as she looks for a way to make a relationship with the transient rodeo star work Summer's not sure she has the fortitude to go on a second date. Can they find love among the tragedy?

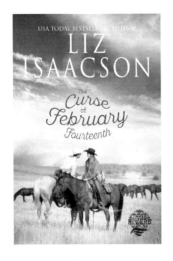

The Curse of February Fourteenth: A Three Rivers Ranch Romance™ (Book 13): Cal Hodgkins, cowboy veterinarian at Bowman's Breeds, isn't planning to meet anyone at the masked dance in small-town Three Rivers. He just wants to get his bachelor friends off his back and sit on the sidelines to drink his punch. But when he sees a woman dressed in gorgeous butterfly wings and cowgirl boots with blue stitching, he's smitten. Too bad she runs away from the dance before he can get her name, leaving only her boot behind...

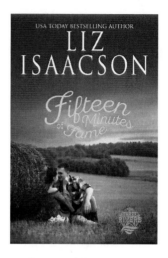

Fifteen Minutes of Fame: A Three Rivers Ranch Romance™ (Book 14): Navy Richards is thirty-five years of tired—tired of dating the same men, working a demanding job, and getting her heart broken over and over again. Her aunt has always spoken highly of the match-maker in Three Rivers, Texas, so she takes a six-month sabbatical from her high-stress job as a pediatric nurse, hops on a bus, and meets with the matchmaker. Then she meets Gavin Redd. He's handsome, he's hardworking, and he's a cowboy. But is he an Aquarius too? Navy's not making a move until she knows for sure...

Sixteen Steps to Fall in Love: A Three Rivers Ranch Romance™ (Book 15): A chance encounter at a dog park sheds new light on the tall, talented Boone that Nicole can't ignore. As they get to know each other better and start to dig into each other's past, Nicole is the one who wants to run. This time from her growing admiration and attachment to Boone. From her aging parents. From herself.

But Boone feels the attraction between them too, and he decides he's tired of running and ready to make Three Rivers his permanent home. **Can Boone and Nicole use their faith to overcome their differences and find a happily-ever-after together?**

The Sleigh on Seventeenth Street: A Three Rivers Ranch Romance™ (Book 16): A cowboy with skills as an electrician tries a relationship with a down-on-her luck plumber. Can Dylan and Camila make water and electricity play nicely together this Christmas season? Or will they get shocked as they try to make their relationship work?

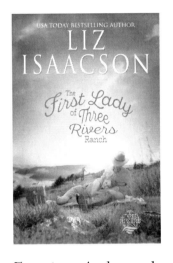

The First Lady of Three Rivers Ranch: A Three Rivers Ranch Romance™ (Book 17): Heidi Duffin has been dreaming about opening her own bakery since she was thirteen years old. She scrimped and saved for years to afford baking and pastry school in San Francisco. And now she only has one year left before she's a certified pastry chef. Frank Ackerman's father has recently retired, and he's taken over the largest cattle ranch in the Texas Panhandle. A horseman through and through, he's also nearing thirty-one and looking for someone to bring love and joy to a homestead that's been dominated by men for a decade. But when he convinces Heidi to come clean the cowboy cabins, she changes all that. But the siren's call of a bakery is still loud in Heidi's ears, even if she's also seeing a future with Frank. Can she rely on her faith in ways she's never had to before or will their relationship end when summer does?

Second Generation in Three Rivers Romance™ Series

Step back into the heartwarming small Texas town of Three Rivers! This beloved town has captured the hearts of 2.5 million readers and caught the eye of Sony Pictures, and now a new generation of cowboys and cowgirls is ready to take center stage. Scan the QR code below with your phone to check out this new series!

1. The Cowboy Who Came Home - featuring Squire's son, Finn from SECOND CHANCE RANCH!

Seven Sons Ranch in Three Rivers Romance™ Series

Meet the cowboy billionaire brothers at Seven Sons Ranch! Scan the QR code below with your phone to check out this complete series.

1. Rhett's Make-Believe Marriage
2. Tripp's Trivial Tie
3. Liam's Invented I-Do
4. Jeremiah's Bogus Bride
5. Wyatt's Pretend Pledge
6. Skyler's Wanna-Be Wife
7. Micah's Mock Matrimony
8. Gideon's Precious Penny

Shiloh Ridge Ranch in Three Rivers Romance™ Series

Meet the cowboy billionaires in the southern hills outside of Three Rivers! Scan the QR code below with your phone to check out this complete series.

About Liz

Liz Isaacson writes inspirational romance, usually set in Texas, or Wyoming, or anywhere else horses and cowboys exist. She lives in Utah, where she writes full-time, takes her two dogs to the park everyday, and eats a lot of veggies while writing. Find her on her website at feelgoodfiction-books.com

Made in United States
North Haven, CT
30 January 2025

65187900R00159